BE SHOT FOR SIXPENCE

An announcement in *The Times* sets Philip on an intriguing trail through Europe. The message is from an old school friend, Colin Studd-Thompson who had instructed the newspaper to publish only if they fail to hear from him. Knowing that Colin is in troubled Europe and involved somehow in Intelligence at first makes Philip disinclined to interfere but circumstances at home are enough to start him on a dangerous and exciting quest.

BE SHOT FOR SIXPENCE

Michael Gilbert

First published 1956
by
Hodder and Stoughton Limited
This edition 1997 by Chivers Press
published by arrangement with
the author

ISBN 0 7540 8503 1

The characters in this book are entirely
imaginary and bear no relation to any
living person.

British Library Cataloguing in Publication Data available

Printed and bound in Great Britain by
Redwood Books, Trowbridge, Wiltshire

CONTENTS

TO
CHRISTOPHER
WHO HAS NOT YET
BEEN LIQUIDATED BY THE QUEEN'S ENEMIES

Part I

SHUFFLE, CUT AND DEAL

" Oh ! who would fight and march and countermarch,
Be shot for sixpence in a battle-field
And shovell'd up into some bloody trench
Where no-one knows ? but let me live my life.

Oh ! who would cast and balance at a desk.
Perch'd like a crow upon a three-legged stool.
Till all his juice is dried, and all his joints
Are full of chalk ? but let me live my life.

Oh ! who would love ?   I woo'd a woman once
But she was sharper than the Eastern wind
And all my heart turned from her, as a thorn
Turns from the sea ; but let me live my life."

Tennyson. 'Audley Court '.

Chapter I

THE RESULT OF TAKING A FIRST CLASS TICKET

I DISLIKE good-byes.

Why should a man invoke the Deity because he is moving his unimportant self from one place to another ?

My cousin Michael, who is used to my habits, takes no offence if I fail to do the conventional thing and I can still enjoy a very occasional week-end with him in his converted rectory in Kent. He is the mildest of men and makes his living by writing thrillers. It is a pleasure to see him at work, seated in what was once the rector's study, gleaming kindly through his horn-rimmed spectacles at the hollyhocks and lupins which frame the croquet lawn; writing in his precise and scholarly hand:

"*'This is a knife, and I know how to use it,' said the thief softly.*"

If a thief with a knife came to the old rectory what would Michael do, I wonder? Put him on to pruning the miles of untidy privet hedge?

Michael has a wife, a small, resolute, woman with the spirit of a grenadier and four fat daughters. I have none of these things. That is why I can only visit him very occasionally, for I am sure to come away disliking myself.

I got up at six o'clock. One of the fat daughters was singing a hymn but otherwise the house was quiet. I made myself some tea and started on the five mile walk to the station through the Kent countryside. The countryside was wide awake; it is only authors and business men who can afford to waste in bed the lovely hours between sunrise and breakfast time.

It took me a little under sixty minutes to reach the station and I was in plenty of time for the eight-three. This, I can only suppose, was the business train. When I got into the first class carriage—(a non-smoker; I have not that particular vice myself and see no reason why I should tolerate it in others)—it was empty. But as we stopped at station after little station it filled up, and I realised that I was in an exclusive sort of club. In fact, I am not sure that I had not stolen the oldest member's seat. The other members were very upset about it.

They settled down after a bit, and took up the conversation, where they had left it off when they got to Victoria the morning before. Being unable to join in I contented myself with studying their faces. There were superficial differences but really they were the same face. The dropped and multiplied chins, the pursed mouths, the eyes which tried to look worldly but succeeded only in looking greedy and frightened. Little, tired eyes of men who spent their working days sitting in swivel chairs in over-heated offices thinking about money. I should have been hard put to it to say which of them I fancied least.

The svelte man in the corner with white hair, pince-nez glasses and an authoritative manner of speaking which he must have picked up from years of laying down the law to people who depended on him for their daily bread. Or the fat man with the pink tip of his nose—a tiny, unheeded, warning light showing what would happen to him if he persisted in absorbing more carbohydrates than his body could burn ; or the military type, with field officer moustache and a velvet coat collar who was repeating, with the tired ferocity of a bilious tiger that all strikers were communists and all communists ought to be shot down. Not shot; shot down. Apparently an important distinction.

"I was lunching with Herbert the other day," said the white haired man, "and he told me, but you'd better not pass it on"—(since I didn't belong to the Club I was presumably supposed to be deaf as well)—"that the Government are contemplating—definitely contemplating—legislation in the next session."

"How do you stop strikes by legislation?" asked the military type.

"Quite simple. By restoring the full legal effect of the contract of service between employer and employee. Then any strike becomes a breach of contract, and the strikers become liable in damages. The damages would have to be paid out of union funds, which would soon be exhausted. No union funds, no strike pay. No strike pay, no strike."

The fat man said that it sounded all right but he didn't mind betting that the Government didn't do it.

"They *must* do it," said the white haired dictator. "Do you know how much my firm lost in the last strike?"

No one knew, so he told them.

A thin man, who had not spoken up till now, said that he saw from his paper that radio active fish were being caught in the Pacific.

They worried about radio active fish until the train got to Victoria.

I walked from Victoria Station to Penny's flat in Paulton's Square. (And if you think that Penny is a silly woman's-magazine sort of name I entirely agree with you. And it is remarkably appropriate to this particular bearer of it).

It was well past nine when I got there and the City boys were streaming out in their bowler hats and striped trousers with all the cares of the world in their brief-cases: but not much sign of life from Penny's flat. I picked up the paper and milk and opened the door with my key and went in.

All the washing up which had accumulated since Friday evening was piled neatly in the kitchen. She was a methodical slut. I contemplated for a moment washing it up myself, but refrained. She would only look at me out of her melting eyes and say, "Oh darling, how *sweet* of you."

I went into the bedroom. She was lying on her side with one pillow in the small of her back and the other under her shoulder and enough of her left breast showing to emphasise the relationship between us. The female breast is not, in itself, in my opinion an attractive sight, least of all at nine o'clock in the morning.

I removed two pairs of stockings from the low chair by the electric fire and sat down.

"Did you have a lovely, lovely week-end?"

"Lovely, lovely."

"All those sweet children. It makes me maternal to think of them. Oughtn't we to start one."

"Right now, do you mean?"

"Well, no. But soon. Then you'd have to make an honest woman of me."

"I have never been able to see where honesty comes into that particular transaction."

" Darling, you sound grumpy."

"I am grumpy."

"Liver?"

"My liver is in perfect order. It just so happens that I travelled up in the train with a carriage full of people, and I started by thinking how terrible they were, and suddenly I wondered if that was what I was going to look like myself in ten years time."

"Were they bloody?"

"Beyond description." I thought for a moment to get them straight in my own mind. "They had neither the disciplined carefulness of professional men nor the undisciplined carelessness of artists. They were foaled by Money out of Timidity. They looked like burst brown paper bags."

"It was your own fault. You should have travelled third class and enjoyed yourself. And for goodness sake stop exaggerating. There's nothing wrong with business men. They were probably quite nice when you got to know them."

"Kind to their families, church wardens and pillars of the local Conservative party."

"Well, what's wrong with people like that? Your father's a church warden *and* a J.P."

"What's my father got to do with it?"

"Look, Philip." She sat up in bed and I knew she was going to say something tricky. "I saw your father on Saturday—"

"You *what*!"

"Don't be angry before I've told you. He asked to see me. I didn't see why not. I think he's very nice."

"For God's sake—"

"He wasn't shocked, or anything like that."

"That's not the point."

I found I was starting to shout, and took a hold of myself.

"What exactly are you trying to do? First you talk of children, and then you rush off to see my family. What are you? An aspiring young bride?"

"Don't be horrid."

"I told you not to see my father."

"He knew all about us."

"He knows all about myxomatosis. But he doesn't want diseased rabbit served up for breakfast."

"Darling. What a horrible thing to say."

"The facts are clear enough anyway. You gave me a promise and you've broken it."

I got up and pulled out my suitcase from behind the wardrobe.

I have very little use for material possessions. I keep a few spare clothes, things like my dinner jacket and my climbing kit, at the Club and I have odd garments and changes of linen scattered about in the houses of friends and relations; never more than will go in a single suitcase. Possessions attach you. Get rid of them and you take a step towards non-attachment.

"What on earth are you doing?"

"Packing. Where did I leave my hairbrushes?"

"Where are you going?"

"Away."

Penny sat up in bed abruptly.

"I believe you're serious," she said.

"Did I leave them in the bathroom? Of course I'm serious."

They were in the bathroom. Also a dirty shirt and some soiled collars and handkerchiefs that I made into a bundle. The Club would be able to get them washed for me.

When I got back Penny was up. She had put on her dressing gown and, first reaction of women to a crisis, had very rapidly but skilfully made up her face.

"Got them," I said. There was just room in the suitcase for everything.

"Darling," she said, and there was an infinite tenderness in her voice. "I've just realised what's happening. I'm dreaming all this, and in a minute I'm going to wake up."

"You'll wake up," I agreed.

"But—"

"The rent's paid to the end of the month. Not that it matters. You've got as much money as I have. This is the end of the instalment, Penny. I said if ever you tried to bring my family into this I'd leave you. You have and I am."

"Is it possible that you're being a little bit of a prig?"

"Quite possible," I said.

"Then you're really going? For ever?"

"For ever," I said. "And ever."

"You're not even going to kiss me?"

"I don't mind," I said, "without prejudice."

Two minutes later I was in the street. I got breakfast at a coffee stall and walked to my club.

"You can have your usual room in the annexe," the Secretary said. "Things are a bit easier now, but if you can give me any idea how long you're likely to want it?"

"A fortnight at the outside," I said.

I should be able to make any arrangements in that time.

At eleven o'clock I rang up the office.

Douglas answered the telephone himself. He seemed cheerful.

"I've just seen Carnwath," he said, "and we've landed the hedge-trimming contract. Six machines, six crews, and one maintenance crew and one stores lorry. The whole outfit to be ready in three months' time."

"That's good isn't it," I said.

"We'll show thirty per cent clear of all overheads."

"That on top of the Belsize contract makes it look like a record year."

"Our only enemy," said Douglas, " is going to be the tax collector." But he said it cheerfully. Douglas is an accountant and enjoys fighting the tax collector. They speak the same language. I don't think we ever do anything actually dishonest, but we seem to pay away less of our profits to the Revenue than any other company I've ever heard of.

"I don't think I shall turn up today."

"That's all right," said Douglas. "Everything's under control. Why don't you help yourself to a holiday."

"I'll think about it," I said.

That was the trouble. Everything *was* under control. I don't want you to get this wrong. Douglas plays absolutely fair with me. He works a twelve-hour day to my six-hour one, and we share every penny of the profits equally. My share brings me more money than I really know how to spend. But the fun has gone out of it.

When I formed the company, just after the War, it was really something. It was based on an idea I'd had that practically no one in the post-war world was going to be able to afford a gardener; or not enough gardeners for the garden they had to keep up. Acres of beds unweeded and lawns going back to rank grass, miles of hedges sprouting and untrimmed.

We started by getting a license for the sale in this country of a cheap American motor-mower. Then we got hold of the first really good automatic mower and weeder. It's a Dutch machine; they built it for their tulip beds, and we adapted it and got a license to manufacture it here.

Boy, did our troubles start then! With the mower we had only been middle-men. That's easy. You can be a middle-man with one room, one typist, and a lot of nerve. But as soon as we started to manufacture we needed real money. That meant going to the City; and it meant debentures and preference shares and unsecured loans and arrangements of all sorts. And that's where I brought Douglas in. I'd met him in the war and I knew he was a teetotaller and a chartered accountant. My impression was that he was an able chap; and I was right.

For four years we hung on by our eyelashes. There were big firms who didn't like us cutting in. And some of them weren't too scrupulous. It was a fight. I didn't work a six-hour day then. Sometimes I didn't get much sleep out of the whole twenty-four.

It was the Combine Hedge Clipper that put us on top. We didn't sell it to people. We hired it to them, with a crew that knew how to work it. Not to small gardens, but big places. It paid very handsomely, and, as often as not, got us the other orders as well.

For some time now, I'd just sat back and let the money come in. I hadn't realised, until that morning, that the whole idea had died on me.

Douglas, of course, wanted to go on. On to bigger and better things. I didn't. I wanted to back-pedal, which, come to think of it, was the situation between me and Penny, too, in a nutshell.

The porter came into the coffee room where I was browsing through the early editions of the evening papers and said that Mrs. Pastonberry was asking for me. He had told her that he would ascertain if I was in the building.

(Mrs. Pastonberry is Penny. Mr. Pastonberry had been a very superior sort of wholesale grocer who had married Penny when she was eighteen and lived just long enough to endow her with his considerable worldly goods before passing away as the result, it was believed, of over-indulgence in his own port).

"I hope that you didn't say I was here."

"Of course not, sir."

Silly question really.

"Well, that's all right. Because I'm not."

I had lunch at the Polidor, rather a lengthy function as I met two people I knew. They had a spare girl with them and we made up a foursome. There was, I thought, a faint look of invitation in the spare girl's eyes when we parted, but I disregarded it and went off to spend the afternoon at the Zoo.

As an antidote to mental disequilibrium there is nothing like the Aquarium. Through warm, uncounted hours I lingered, staring across the glass frontier into another world. A world of strange dimensions where Time did not exist, and it was as easy to go upwards and backwards as it was forwards and downwards. A frightening world where dwelt Esox Lucius, the Pike and Maia Maia the spider crab. A world of shadows and half-lights in which you might encounter bustling little characters like the Trigger Fish and the Schoolmaster Snapper, witless oafs like Dollo's lung fish or, for plain horror, Silurus, the Giant Catfish, who sits white eyed in the shadow of his rocky chamber, his thick whiskers trembling as he dreams of ancient evil.

When I got back to the Club the porter said, "Mrs. Pastonberry called, sir."

"She actually came here?"

"Yes, sir."

"What did you do with her?"

"We put her in the small committee room."

"That was rather drastic. How long did she survive?"

"She left approximately forty minutes later, sir."

"She's tougher than I thought."

The small committee room is a terrible apartment. It contains two hundred volumes of *Punch*, which have been specially bound for the club in half-yearly numbers in black buckram with the club's crest on the spine; a buffalo's head with one eye, and no windows of any sort. Even bailiffs have been removed from it screaming in less than thirty minutes.

I went up to dress for dinner.

In the morning, Penny telephoned again.

This time, for a change, I decided I would take the call. She sounded cross.

"I tried three times to get hold of you yesterday," she said.

"I got the messages," I said.

"I don't believe you were out at all."

"I assure you I was. I went to the Zoo in the afternoon and the Crazy Gang in the evening."

"Stop behaving like a fool."

"What do you suggest I do?"

"Come back here, of course."

"Penny," I said. "You're not trying. I told you. Remember? I'm not coming back."

"Well come out from behind that terrible Club so that I can get hold of you."

"One of the reasons men belong to Clubs is to protect them from people like you."

"That bloody porter. When I ring up now he sounds just as if he thought I was a tart."

"Well—" I said, diplomatically.

The slam of the receiver going back nearly deafened me.

I retired to the morning room and opened *The Times*. There was no need to hurry. If Douglas wanted me for anything he could ring me.

The first thing I saw was the advertisement. It was at the top of the Personal Column and it said "Attention, Philip. If you want to know the inner story, go to Twickenham and see Henry. Colin."

It was for all the world as if one of the figures in Madame Tussauds had stepped smartly from its dais, raised its head, and addressed me by name.

I sat for a few minutes, staring at it, in an idiotic way as if I hoped the letters might themselves say something. I even cast my eye down the column to see if there might be anything further addressed to me; but this was the only one.

"Attention, Philip—"

I went over to the rack where the back numbers were stored. It was in Monday's paper too. I must have been too pre-occupied to notice it. Monday was the first time though. I went back through several weeks to make sure of that.

Then I put on my hat and went out quickly.

The commissionaire in the glass hutch at the top of the stairs asked me, with all the courtesy for which this great newspaper is famous, if I would be good enough to wait. He showed me into a cubicle which had the air of an exceptionally well appointed confessional, and said that Mr. Satterley would be along soon.

In due course Mr. Satterley appeared. He was tiny. Smaller even than me and I am no size at all. A humming bird of a man. Neat, bright and poised.

"You came about an announcement in our Personal Column," he said.

"That's right, it's one which appeared today. Yesterday too, I believe."

I took out the copy of the paper and showed it to him.

Mr. Satterley said, "And you are interested in Axminster carpets?"

"Not that one. The one before. The first one in the column."

" Oh, yes?"

"I wondered if you could tell me anything about it."

"There is not usually a great deal to tell," said Mr. Satterley, politely. "We usually accept such—er—announcements, by post. Provided that they seem to us to be genuine, and not objectionable in any way—you'd be surprised how often they contain a 'double entendre'—we really become quite expert at spotting them."

"I don't think this one is a leg-pull," I said.

"No. No. It certainly seemed genuine."

We didn't seem to be getting anywhere.

Nevertheless it seemed to me that Mr. Satterley was stalling. He had not said, right out, as he easily could have done, "*This* announcement was sent by post." I felt that the time had come to abandon finesse.

"Do you know anything about the person who put this one in?"

"I'm afraid," said Mr. Satterley, "that I must ask you a question in return. What is your interest in the matter?"

"I can answer that without any difficulty. I have every reason to suppose that I am the Philip to whom the message is addressed and, if I am right about that it was put in by Colin Studd-Thompson."

"Studd-Thompson. Yes."

"Did he come here with it himself?"

"Yes, he did." Mr. Satterley looked at me over his glasses and added, "I knew Mr. Studd-Thompson very well, of course."

I nodded. I was aware of Colin's connection with the

Times. One of his uncles, or maybe great uncles, had been a distinguished foreign editor.

"He instructed me that if anyone came to inquire about the advertisement, claiming to be the Philip to whom it was addressed, I was to ask him a question."

"Ask away."

"I was to ask who Henry was."

"That's easy," I said. "Henry is a woman. A charming and accomplished person of uncertain age who was at one time governess to Colin and his brother. Later on she was a governess in our family. We called her Henry because she was the eighth."

"The psychology of young children is a fascinating study," said Mr. Satterley.

He took off his glasses, polished them with little, darting, movements, replaced them securely on his nose and said: "How can I help you?"

"I'm not too sure. To start with, it was news to me that Colin had been in England lately."

"I'm afraid that does not follow. This announcement was delivered to us—let me see—more than two months ago. Nearer three."

"Then how did it come to be put in on this particular date?"

"Our instructions were, that if we did *not* hear from Mr. Studd-Thompson by the last day of any week, we were to insert the announcement during the whole of the week following."

In silence I tried to think this out. Silence so absolute that I could suddenly hear a woman speaking quite clearly two rooms away. She was accepting an announcement for the Births Column and seemed to be making heavy going of it.

"I take it, then," I said at last, "that when he failed to get through to you——"

"We heard from him regularly for nine weeks."

"So you know where he is—or was?"

"I'm afraid not. The messages were sent through our foreign correspondents. The last three came from Rome—

but that does not mean that Mr. Studd-Thompson was necessarily in Italy."

"I see. And last Friday—or Saturday—you got no message at all—"

"That is correct."

"It may have been delayed."

"Possibly. Our messages are not often delayed. And in any event our instructions were categoric. If we had not heard by midnight on Saturday, the announcement had to be inserted on Monday—and for the five days following."

"G-o-t-t—" said the shrill voice.

"It is really rather a remarkable circumstance," went on Mr. Satterley. "Owing to the peculiar way in which this matter has been arranged you are probably the only person in England who is in a position to find out exactly what has happened to Mr. Studd-Thompson."

"—f-r-i-e-d. That's right. As in fried bread."

"Yes," I said. "Well, I'm very much obliged to you."

Chapter II

TWICKENHAM AND SLOANE SQUARE

I WALKED back slowly, and rather blindly, along the Embankment. My feet took me into the little garden by Temple Station. I don't know its name. It's an austere place, full of office sandwich eaters at lunch time but deserted for the rest of the day; guarded at one end by John Stuart Mill and at the other by William Edward Forster.

I settled my body carefully down on a seat facing the Embankment and allowed my mind to drift backwards for ten, for twenty, for thirty years. . . .

Myself as a new boy at a preparatory school on the South Coast. Serials in the *Boy's Own Paper* had prepared me for the worst. I see now, looking back, that everyone was enormously kind and considerate, but to go from home, at the age of eight, and into exile, for the eternity of three months in a strange world; it must always be such a parting as will make the other partings of life seem unimportant.

Colin had been the first person to speak to me. He had spoken with the patronage demanded by his superior position (for he had already been at the school for a whole term) but he had spoken kindly. The train was passing Three Bridges. He waved at a grassy knoll behind the town and said, without preamble: "Did you know they had a battle there during the Civil War, in 1640?" I said that I had not known. As the train thundered south (if such an expression can be applied to the progress of the old London Brighton and South Coast Railway) Colin told me a number of other surprising things. Soon we were friends. I cannot remember how soon, for no doubt Colin had his dignity to consider and I was remarkably unsociable, even as a boy; but friends we became.

It proved to be almost the only genuine, lasting friendship

of my life and I have no doubt that psychologists would have given themselves headaches trying to explain it. There wasn't an ounce of sentiment in it; or, if a little of this necessary lubricant must be present, then no more than the barest drop. I think the truth is that we suited each other, like two old club men who enjoy each other's company on the basis that they will respect each other's foibles and listen charitably to each other's reminiscences.

We went to different public schools and to different Universities, and saw, of course, a good deal less of each other thereafter. But whenever we did meet we seemed to pick up matters exactly where we had laid them down. (Only a few months before, happening to be walking through the Middle Temple, I heard a bland voice behind me saying "The building is eighteenth century, and shockingly proportioned, but the foundation is four centuries older," and I knew, without looking round, that Colin was back in England).

It had always been like that. The middle of the Long Vacation. A ring at the door bell, Colin's gentle voice, so curiously at variance with his craggy face (in a dim light, not unlike the First Murderer in Ben Greet's open-air production of Macbeth). "You must come along, Philip. Such an interesting little man. A Lithuanian. His mother was murdered by the White Russians and his father starved to death under the Red sort—I rode *all* round London yesterday with him on the top of a bus."

It was all very well for Colin. He was reading modern languages—and already spoke half a dozen of them with alarming fluency. I should have been as tongue tied with his Lithuanian as his Lithuanian would have been bored with me.

Colin gravitated naturally to the Diplomatic and I knew that he had served spells at Belgrade and Budapest, and had been in Germany so late in August 1939 that he had finally been forced to quit it, in the early hours of the morning, and on foot, at Singen.

During the war he had been withdrawn from regular work and I should have known, if I had not been too busy

to spare it a thought, that he must have been with Intelligence. His background and proclivities made it a certainty.

I got to my feet and walked slowly down the garden. I
needed the incentive of movement to get my brain working.
Like an old car on a cold morning, it works quite well, but
I have to start it off down a slope.

My strongest feeling, and I must confess it now, was a
very marked disinclination to interfere. Colin had clearly
got himself involved in' some business inside the troubled
perimeter of Europe, and it must be business with an
Intelligence slant to it.

To the man in the street, who knows absolutely nothing
about it, the notion of Intelligence is a not unpleasant one.
I know very little more than the man in the street, but certain
of my war-time experiences (which I will mention in their
proper place) had made me wary. Though far from realising
exactly what went on behind the discreet façade of those
offices in Sloane Square and Buckingham Palace Road, I
was past the honeymoon stage of my acquaintanceship with
the Secret Service.

My other reason was a very slight distrust of Colin's
motives. He had a medieval love of craft-for-crafts-sake.
If he had wanted to meet me during the school holidays his
normal procedure was to ring up a friend and ask him to
telephone me and tell me that if I went to an address in
Pentonville I would find a note telling me what to do next.
That was the way his mind worked. No doubt it earned him
high marks in the Diplomatic but it made everyday life
a little complicated.

However, there was no need to commit myself yet. The
first step was clearly marked. Since I alone knew who Henry
was, I must go and see Henry. That would be a pleasure. I
had been meaning to look her up for some time. When I had
heard what she had to say would be the time to make my
mind up about the next move.

That settled, I again got to my feet. A little man with a
long nose got up from the seat next to me and moved off in
the opposite direction.

I started out for Twickenham after lunch, and I went on foot. I enjoy walking and am not one of those who has to put on fancy dress and go all the way to Teviotdale or Exmoor before I can enjoy myself.

I remember once—it was after my break with Eileen—I started out from Curzon Street at two o'clock in the morning, in the clothes I happened to have on at the time, and walked to Inverness. My dancing pumps finally fell to pieces at Doncaster and I replaced them by a pair of gym shoes. (It's a fallacy that you can't walk in gym shoes. If your feet are in good condition they are excellent foot gear for made-up roads).

I find that a fairly fast rate suits me. With a detour across the rough in Richmond Park I covered ten miles in well under two hours. Green Gables, Barkas Road, is on the outskirts of Twickenham. It is a nice little house, in a road of nice little houses. I know what it cost because six of us clubbed together to buy it for Henry when she retired. That was before the war. I would have cost us a great deal more now.

Henry opened the door. She was a neat, spare, fierce figure, with the uprightness which, in this decadent age, is attributed only to Royalty.

"I've walked down to see you," I said.

"You've walked! All the way from London?"

"It's not very far."

"You're sure you haven't walked yourself into a damp sweat."

"I'm not sweating at all," I said, indignantly.

"I could lend you a dressing-gown."

"No, really. I'm as dry as a bone. I hardly hurried at all."

"You're always in a hurry." She laid her old hand inside my coat, over my heart. "I'll let it go this time. Come in."

We went into the back room, which looked through French windows onto a square of garden. It was as neat as any room could be which contained (I once counted them) forty eight framed and six unframed photographs. Most of them were boys and young men. Boys in shorts and sweaters and blazers and school caps and young men in blazers and sweaters and shorts—and in the dress and undress uniform of a dozen different Regiments of Foot Guards, Lancers and Hussars. Mostly they were private photographs, but there was one I had not seen before, cut from one of the glossy magazines.

"That's Victor," she said.

I remembered Victor, a thin, whitefaced boy.

"A bundle of nerves," said Henry. "The time I had with him. Night after night. If I could get him to sleep by ten o'clock I was lucky." The picture showed him on his way to the palace to receive his V.C.

"How did last winter go?" I asked, as I settled carefully down in one of her high backed chairs. ("Don't slouch, Master Philip. It weakens the spine.").

"Terrible," said Henry. "France and Ireland were here. Neither of them good matches. No Calcutta Cup and no Welsh match. That's the match I like. Right from the start. You should see the little men in cloth caps run out and tie the leeks on to the cross bars, and the policemen chase them."

I agreed that the Welsh match was fun. "But still, you had the seven-a-sides."

"I expect it was Colin you came to talk about," said Henry, suddenly. "Rugger's not really your game. You might have made a scrum half if you'd been a bit wider in the hips."

"I expect that's because I didn't always sit up straight at table," I said. "Yes, it was about Colin."

"Have the advertisements started?"

"They started yesterday."

Henry looked steadily at me, but said nothing. If I hadn't been sure before, I knew now that Colin was her real favourite. Above Aubrey, who got so near to the top of Everest; above Victor, for all his V.C.; and a long way above me.

" Show it me," she said.

I took the cutting out of my pocket and passed it across. She read it carefully. Her old eyes scorned spectacles.

"A pity," was all she said.

"I expect you'd better tell me what he said."

"It was four months ago. I'd just got back from watching

the Harlequins play Oxford, and I found him waiting on my doorstep. He looked a little fatter than usual, but otherwise just the same. He never changes."

I nodded. Colin's craggy face settled into its adult mould when he was about fifteen and has remained practically unchanged since.

"Whilst I was boiling the kettle for tea he told me what he'd been up to. "You're quite right, Henry," he said. "I *am* getting fat. It's because I do nothing but sit still, in a fairy palace, waiting for something to happen. It's quite exciting, but it doesn't alter the fact that I have to do a lot of sitting still, and too much eating, and too much drinking."

"Then, when we were having tea, he told me something else. I can't remember it exactly—not word for word—but what he said was this. "It's not my show. I'm only in it as a guest artist, I've got no standing at all. And it's so secret that I don't suppose there's anything more secret in the world today. That's why I'm telling you as little as I can."

Henry broke off and gave one of her dry laughs. "You know why he said that to me? Once when he was very small, he came along to me and said "I know a tremendous secret. I'll tell it you if you like," and I said: "Certainly not. If it's a secret you mustn't tell anyone." He was terribly deflated, but he hadn't forgotten it. Have another crumpet?"

"I oughtn't to," I said, "but I will."

"You take as much interest in your figure as a ballerina. Well, then he told me about the advertisement. "I've got to do it that way," he said. "Because that way doesn't leave any possible line that anyone else in the world can follow up. I told you, it isn't my secret. That's why I've got to be so careful." Supposing he doesn't see it," I said. "That's a chance I've got to take," said Colin. "But it's not a serious one. I'll let it run for a week. It'll catch his eye all right." And so it did."

"So it did," I said. "What message did he leave?"

"You're to go to Cologne, and walk across the Hohen-zollern Bridge. Be in the middle of the bridge, leaning over the parapet, looking down-river at nine o'clock in the morning."

"Nothing more?"

"It seemed quite clear to me," said Henry. "Now that I've told it to you, I've no need to remember it any more. In fact, I've forgotten it already."

It was true. The information was now mine and mine alone. I do not believe that any power on earth would have extracted it from Henry before, and when she said that she was going to forget it, that was true too. She could control her memory as rigidly as she had controlled everything else in her Spartan life.

"Have one of those cakes," said Henry. "Gateaux, the shops call them. I can't think why. They look just like cakes to me."

I left Barkas Road at six and since I had a dinner date at eight I decided against walking back and made for the Underground station.

Near the entrance to the platform I almost bumped into a little man with a long nose.

The dinner was with a girl called Marianne, but as she doesn't come into this story, all I need say about her is that her estimate of the value of her virtue was much higher than mine, so I was back at the Club shortly after eleven.

The porter said, somewhat apologetically, "Mrs. Pastonberry has been on the telephone twice, sir."

"Did she leave a message?"

"She wanted you to ring her back."

"Well—it's a little late."

"She did say, sir, that it was important. And she told me to tell you, that it was not about herself."

"That sounds unlike Mrs. Pastonberry," I said. "However—"

When she answered I got a surprise. I have heard Penny in all sorts of moods before, but I have never, till then, heard her frightened.

" Darling," she said. "Thank goodness you rang. What *have* you been doing?"

"What do you mean?"

"Do you mean to say you don't know? I've had a man round here all this afternoon asking me the most terrible questions."

"And I've no doubt you gave him some terrible answers."

"It's no laughing matter. He was from M.I.5."

"Are you sure?"

"Of course I'm sure. There've been so many bogus gas inspectors about lately that I made him sit right down whilst I rang up the police. He was genuine all right. I say?"

"Yes."

"You're *not* a spy, are you?"

That's a question I defy anyone to answer with a straight yes or no. "Look here," I said. "I'm very sorry you've been put through this—"

"Well, in a way it was rather exciting. It's you I was thinking about. I didn't tell him a thing."

"That doesn't surprise me," I said. "Because you know absolutely nothing to tell."

"Now you're being horrid again."

I rang off before the quarrel could develop.

I was furious with myself, for my stupidity. Of course the authorities would know about the advertisement even if (lacking the one piece of knowledge that mattered) they could not follow up. It had not been difficult to identify me as Philip—it was no secret that I was one of Colin's oldest friends. And equally obvious I should rush round to Printing House Square as soon as I read the thing.

All they had to do was to have a little man hang round the entrance, armed with my photograph, and follow me when I came out.

I would lead him straight to Henry.

And I had!

Or had I? Come to think of it, little long-nose hadn't shown up in Barkas Road. On the contrary, when I ran into him again he was hanging, rather forlornly, round Twickenham

Station. Well, that one would keep for tomorrow. I was for bed.

Immediately after breakfast I put on my hat and walked out of the Club, down the steps by the Duke of York's column, and along into Green Park. I walked quite slowly and I didn't trouble to look behind me. I knew I should be followed.

It was a different man, and new on the job, I thought. After all, I had seen long-nose twice without taking much notice of him. This one looked like a retired Sergeant Major and clamoured for attention. When I moved, he moved ten paces behind me. When I sat down, he did likewise. As soon as I was sure of him I walked over and sat down beside him.

"At ease," I said. "I'd like a word with you."

"I'm afraid—"

"Let's not worry about all that. All I want from you is some information."

"Who—"

"I want to see your boss in the—what would it be— Foreign Office? Technically I suppose I could go and ring the front door bell and ask for the Foreign Secretary, but I feel sure that I should only be shunted from Department to Department, and waste the whole morning. What I want from you is the name and room number of the man who's interested in my 'case'."

"I'm afraid I don't know what you're talking about."

"Then you're just not trying," I said. "If you won't let me have the name I'm going to call that policeman and report you for molesting me. You won't get a bouquet from the Department for that."

I saw doubt in his eye.

"Really, sir. I can't—"

"Just the name."

"It's most irregular."

The policeman was approaching.

"You might find that Captain Forestier was the man you wanted."

"Where does he hang out?"

"96 Sloane Square."

"I'm obliged to you," I said. I got up, made my way into
Piccadilly and caught a bus. The Sergeant Major was still
devotedly following me. He got on to the same bus and went
upstairs. (Standard technique number one, for lulling your
quarry's suspicions). I felt that the least I could do was to
pay his fare, and I did so.

96 Sloane Square looked like all other small office blocks.
There were the plates of a number of professional firms and
a porter, in a hutch, reading the Continental Edition of the
Daily Mail.

"I want to see a Captain Forestier," I said.

"Which firm would that be, sir?"

"I'm afraid I don't know."

"Well, that makes it a bit difficult," said the porter.
"There's five of 'em—not counting the Company that stores
sports goods in the basement."

I looked at the board. From Kyle and Coppit, Chartered
Surveyors on the ground floor to Theobald Whittlesea
Belize and Partners on the fourth floor all seemed equally
straightforward and equally blameless.

"You wouldn't be in the trade?" said the porter. "Carbons,
paper, drawing pins and such."

"Certainly not," I said. "And if I had been, I can tell you
I shouldn't be dithering round here. I should have said I
wanted to see Mr. Kyle of Kyle and Coppit and walked
straight on up."

"That's right," said the porter. "So you would. Bags of
go, those chaps. But Captain Forestier—I'd help you if I
could. What line's he in?"

"Well, I think it's some sort of security."

"Security?"

It meant nothing to him. I might just as well have said
"Door handles."

I had a sudden inspiration. I looked out into the street. Sure
enough the Sergeant Major was still there. He was gazing
into a shop window (technique number two).

"Which floor?" I shouted.

He looked at me reproachfully, then raised his hand with four fingers and thumb extended.

I went back. "Fith floor, "I said.

"Oh, *them*," said the porter. "They're new. Haven't even put a plate up yet. Some sort of Civil Servants. Security, you said?"

"That's right."

"Well!" He shook his head. "You take the lift to the fourth, then you got to walk."

"I expect I can manage one floor," I said.

I got out of the lift on to the fourth story landing, which was close carpeted, and was presumably the joint property of Mr. Theobald, Mr. Whittlesea, the two Mr. Belizes and their partners. None of them were in evidence. On my left a narrow flight of stairs, covered with new brown linoleum. I went up the stairs, and through a swing door which said "Enter."

At a table, thumbing severely through a Telephone Directory, was a very young lady with brown hair, a tip tilted nose and a mouth full of lovely, toothpaste advertisement teeth. The newspaper she had been reading before she heard me coming was inaccurately hidden behind her chair.

"Yes?" she said, invitingly.

"Yes, indeed," I said. "I mean, I wanted to see Captain Forestier."

"Had you an appointment?"

"Half-past ten. I'm afraid I'm a few minutes late."

She started off gaily towards one of the doors, then frowned, and came back and said, "I'm always forgetting things. I should have asked your name".

"I have no name," I said severely. "Only a number."

Her great saucer eyes grew even larger. If she'd actually been a kitten that would have been the moment I would have picked her up and given her stomach a little tickle.

"97259. And it won't have escaped your notice that it's a number divisible by 7. That means that I have killed a man with my bare hands."

A shade of doubt clouded her face. She walked away, as

haughtily as a girl of her build can walk, and knocked at one
one of the doors. A crisp voice said "Come in." She went in;
the door shut. Almost at once it opened again. She was
furious. It made her look even more like a kitten.

Before she could start I said, "He doesn't know me. All
right. Tell him it's about an advertisement in *The Times*.
Go on. Go on. He can't bite you."

She looked doubtful, opened the door again, went in.
More voices. Quite a lot of talk. Then she reappeared.

"Don't tell me," I said. "Now he *does* want to see me."

As I went past her the temptation to tickle her became
almost overmastering. I mastered it and walked in.

Captain Forestier got up as I came in. He did not come
forward and shake hands nor did he offer me an easy chair.
Not a chummy sort of man, I suspected. He had a brick
red face under startlingly light, reddish hair, and light blue
eyes. He was in mufti, but I am quite certain that his medal
ribbons could have stretched from here to there.

"Well?"

It was a voice which had made roomfuls of recruits jump
to attention.

"What about asking me to sit down?" I said.

He never batted an eyelid.

"I'll ask you to sit down when I think you've got anything
to say to me."

"Don't be silly," I said. There was only one spare chair in
the room, so I annexed it. "If you hadn't thought that I
might have something to say to you, you'd never have let
me in. Little Pussykin would have told a white lie and said
you were in conference."

He flexed himself once or twice on the balls of his feet,
like an athlete who's about to go for a standing jump record,
and said, "I'll give you three minutes."

I resisted the temptation to say "You'll give me just as
long as it takes." There was no sense in annoying him
unnecessarily. I said, "I'm Philip."

"I see." The Captain lowered himself very cautiously into
his chair, as if he expected it to bite him, and said, in a very

c

slightly less aggressive voice: "Good of you to come round. Incidentally, why here?"

"I asked your bloodhound. The second one."

"And he told you?"

"Under duress. I threatened to report him for molesting me."

"And was he?"

"Not actually molesting, no. But he's been following me about all this morning. Yesterday it was your other bloodhound. The small one, with the long nose. He was much better at it. He picked me up in Printing House Square, and followed me down to Twickenham—or did he?"

"I'm afraid you walked him off his feet. He had to give up at Kew."

"How very unenterprising. He could have taken a taxi."

"Not across Richmond Park."

"Provoking. So you still don't know who Henry is."

"I expect we shall locate him in due course," said Captain Forestier, very smoothly. "But it really doesn't matter now, as you had the good sense to come straight to us."

"Fair enough," I said. "Now suppose you tell me what it's all about."

"I'm afraid that's quite impossible," said Captain Forestier, seriously.

I controlled myself.

"Is Studd-Thompson officially involved?"

"No. And even if he had been—"

"You can trust him, but you can't trust me. Is that it?"

"I'm sure Studd-Thompson is an excellent man in his own line," said the Captain. "But he wasn't in my department. He was only on loan to us, you know, from the Foreign Service."

The way in which this was said made several things absolutely plain to me. First, that as a dyed-in-the-wool Intelligence operative he resented having a stray character from the Foreign Service wished on to him; secondly that Colin had already managed to put his back up; thirdly that he regarded Colin's advertisement as something between a howling indiscretion and actual treason; and fourthly and lastly that he loved me not at all, but was prepared to tag along with me just long enough to see whether I was going to be a good boy or another Colin. It's remarkable what a trained Secret Service man can give away in a couple of sentences.

"Tell me something," I said. "I suppose this is all pretty confidential."

He looked at me as if he hardly believed in my existence. Then he said: "You don't know a lot about this sort of thing do you?"

"I did get mixed up in it once," I said. "Not enough to teach me anything, except to dislike it."

He said in a much more friendly voice: "The real trouble is, no one ever tells anyone else the truth about anything. You get a project"—he laid his big hand on the table; the fur on the back of it was like a fox's pelt—"say four people know about it. It might be two in the Pentagon and two in Whitehall. But when they start to work it out they've got to tell other people. So they tell them a story. Not the truth. They bring in other people; and the other people get told a second story. And so on. Even by the time *I* get it, it's probably been wrapped up three or four times."

His fingers picked up a glass-backed hand blotter, which was lying North and South on the desk and turned it accurately ninety degrees so that it lay East and West.

"And which story does Colin know?"

"I hope," he said seriously, "that he doesn't know the truth."

"Because that would make him vulnerable?"

He just looked at me.

"And that's why—wherever he's got to—you don't want me blundering about after him."

"I'll go further than that. You're a sensible chap. You wouldn't have come along here if you hadn't been sensible. So I can tell it to you right out. You mustn't interfere. No question of discretion. You just mustn't do it. It's forbidden."

"What happens," I said, breathing a bit harder, "if I refuse to recognise your right to give me orders?"

"Oh, I don't suppose it will come to that."

"But answer my question. What are you going to do? Imprison me in the Tower?"

"Might do. It's a bit crowded at the moment."

"All right," I said. I climbed out of the chair. Captain Forestier got up too. He had his back to the light and I found it hard to read the expression on his face. He said: "I judge you to be an obstinate man. Don't go rushing into this simply *because* you've been told not to. Of all the silly reasons for doing a thing I should think that would be about the silliest."

"I'll bear it in mind," I said.

Kittypuss was waiting at her desk. The newspaper was more efficiently hidden this time.

"Seven o'clock at the Café de Paris," I said.

She started to look haughty but the effort was too much for her and suddenly all her beautiful teeth shone out, like the sun from behind a Western cloud.

"You'd be pretty surprised if I took you at your word," she said.

"Get a late pass from the boss," I said, "and try."

Chapter III

COLOGNE AND STEINBRUCK

THE seduction of Kittypuss (whose name proved to be Dorinda) proceeded along the most orthodox lines.

She turned up at the Café de Paris all right. Ten minutes after the time I had mentioned, and was she surprised to see me? (She just happened to have been passing that way. A chance in a million!) So we had dinner together and she talked about her home in the country, her sisters, her dogs, and her old mother. We drank half a bottle of white wine between us.

Two or three days later we had dinner again, and this time we got outside a whole bottle of Burgundy. She talked about summer holidays in France and winter holidays in Switzerland.

The next night we started with sherry, knocked back a bottle of Mouton Rothschild, and went on to the Old Pluperfect, in Curzon Street, to dance. I had mentioned, casually that we might be going there, and was delighted to observe the Sergeant Major, in a rather tight dinner jacket, at a table in the corner. She talked about her ambitions, which centred at the moment on running a very select antique shop in Knightsbridge; and I gave her a fatherly kiss in the taxi on the way home.

I'm not sure, but I think the Sergeant Major was in a taxi behind us.

Shortly after that I invited her to my flat. Just a drink, you understand. We'll go on somewhere afterwards. I suggested two nights ahead. She sounded a little thoughtful about this one, but in the end she came back and said bravely, all right, she'd love to. (That's the girl. You'll get promotion for this.)

I said, evening dress, and that will leave us free to do what we like afterwards.

She said, that sounded topping.

Next morning I rang up Douglas, from a call box, and dictated a letter over the telephone to his secretary. It was a letter which I wanted sent straight away to an engineering firm in Brussels who were very closely connected with us in business. They were not exactly a subsidiary, but we honoured each other's cheques.

The address of the flat I had given Dorinda was 2A, Nightcrow Court, which is a big white soulless block north of the Park, on the unfashionable side of Queen's Road. It is known, I believe, as the bailiffs' nightmare because there are so many ways out of it. I have never owned a flat there, but my cousin Cedric has one on the ground floor. (What value he gets for the exorbitant rent he pays is doubtful. He spends his time looking for new varieties of rock plants, and as the ones he cherishes most grow near the tops of the furthest peaks of Asia Minor, Nightcrow Court sees but little of him.) The flat is furnished in execrable taste, and I have a key.

In the afternoon I went for a quiet walk, and when I was quite certain that no one could be following me I hailed a taxi and drove to a small booking agents, near Victoria. I had made use of their services before and was well known to them. The man behind the counter looked slightly surprised at my request.

"I didn't know you were interested in Cathedrals, Major," he said.

"Passionately."

"It'll be mostly old women."

"Next to Cathedrals I like old women best."

"It's your life," he said, "Forty bob with lunch, tea and tips. Dear at half the price."

I paid him in notes and returned to my Club, where I spent the evening losing money in rather a hot bridge school. That was Wednesday.

Thursday dawned bright and fair. I rose early, put on the sort of suit that men about town wear when they are going out of town for the day, and had a hearty breakfast. After break-

fast I cashed a fair sized cheque at the Club desk: (I had been
careful not to go near my bank since my interview with
Captain Forestier).

One final duty remained. I rang up Tony Hancock at the
Alpine Club and told him that I should not be able to give my
promised talk on the North Face of the Creag Meagaidh.
Tony sounded peeved. "I'm terribly sorry," I said, "but I've
been called away."

"It's a girl."

"It's not a girl. It's a far more absorbing and complicated
thing than sex. In fact, I'm giving up a snip of a girl in order
to do it."

"If you're giving up a girl," said Tony "it must be absorbing. How am I going to find a lecturer at this time of
day?"

"Ask Prendergast," I said. "He's been trying for years to
give you his talk about how he climbed Pwillheli."

Tony said something unkind about Prendergast and something even more unkind about me, so I rang off.

I collected a light raincoat, although it had never looked
less like rain, and stepped out. I don't think I was followed
that morning. After all, provided I behaved myself, they had
something better to do than follow me round indefinitely.

However, I didn't take any chances. It cost me sixty
minutes and five changes to reach Buckingham Palace Road,
but by the time I got there I was sure that I was on my own.
And there she was; drawn up at the kerb. A handsome, yellow
twenty-four seater. A placard in front said Know Your
Cathedrals. And a card in the slot said Today's Trip:
Canterbury. A hatchet-faced man was standing with his head
out of the open top and there were twenty three people
already seated. The booking agent had been perfectly right.
They were all women.

We got to Canterbury in time for lunch. It was a lovely
drive. I shared my seat with a schoolmistress and stood her a
coffee when we stopped for a break at Rochester. She had
visited every Cathedral in England and Wales. Some of them
twice.

Before we went in to lunch I had a word with the hatchet-faced organiser, and told him that I had friends in Canterbury who might be putting me up for the night. Not to worry if I wasn't there when the bus started. He promised not to worry. He looked like a man who didn't worry much.

There was a local train from Canterbury to Dover which didn't leave until three. It was going to mean cutting it a bit fine the other end, but at least it gave me plenty of time in Canterbury to do my shopping.

I decided that a suitcase looked more respectable than a rucksack. I'd have liked to get a second-hand one, but that proved impossible. So I compromised with a large, cheap, fibre job. I reckoned if I banged it about a bit it wouldn't look too glaringly new. Then I fitted myself out with some shorts and pyjamas and underclothes and shaving gear and things of that sort. I had brought my sponge bag with me in my pocket, and that, at any rate, looked authentically old and used. I was lucky enough to pick up a second-hand tweed jacket at a little shop in a street behind the market.

I unfolded and refolded everything a few times. Most of the stuff still looked rather new, but it would have to do.

I got out at Dover Priory Station with barely twenty minutes in hand. Luckily there was a taxi waiting and it scooted me downhill to the Marine Station. I hurried across the footbridge, and onto the platform. The tail end of the queue from the boat train was still moving. I tacked myself onto it.

I had my boat ticket. Douglas had got it for me from an ordinary travel agency three days before. Passport stamped. Customs. Everyone in a hurry. Nobody really looked at anything. No questions. The policeman at the turnstile gave me the curious, ruminative stare which policemen always give you when they are thinking of something else.

The gangways came up. The ship's hooter let out a mournful blast, and I sank into a deck chair. As we swung away, stern first, from the quay, I saw that it was exactly half-past four. By eight o'clock Dorinda would be knocking at the door of my flat. She would be furiously angry, bitterly disappointed, and deeply relieved that the ultimate sacrifice was not required of her.

The Sergeant Major might get a night's rest, too.

" Tea in the salon," said the white coated waiter.

"The sea looks smooth," I said.

"Of the smoothest," said the waiter.

I was glad of that. I am no sailor.

Before the war you used to reach Cologne, on this route, at midnight. The new Saphir-Express will get you there in time for dinner. However, I had one important call to make, so I stepped off at Brussels, where I spent an uncomfortable night at a second-class hotel in the quarter behind the station. I was fairly certain that I had made a clean getaway but there was no sense in taking unnecessary risks.

In the morning I called on our Brussels associates to pick up the money I had asked for, most of it in German marks, and by lunch time I was in Cologne.

I had the afternoon to kill, so I walked about a bit before choosing an hotel. The Koenig seemed about my mark. It was a modest place, with only half a dozen bedrooms and a big downstairs bar with a tiled stove, a zinc counter with a beer engine, and a few well scrubbed tables.

I had my evening meal there, saw a very bad film, and slept like a log.

I had asked to be called at seven, and by half-past eight I had breakfasted and paid my bill. I told the proprietor that I was not certain whether I should be staying another night, but if he was agreeable, perhaps I might leave my luggage with him until I had made my plans.

This was a mistake, but not one I could have foreseen.

A minute later I was in the street, heading for the Rhine.

It was a lovely morning. A brisk breeze was packing away the clouds and snapping the flags. The customary Trade Fair was in progress and Cologne was full of flags. Even the grim battered hulk of the Cathedral had life and colour that morning.

My watch said seven minutes to nine as I set foot on the Hohenzollern bridge. It was built for the railway, but it carries as a sort of afterthought a sidewalk, outside the main structure, for bicyclists and pedestrians.

I had no difficulty in finding the exact place. The bridge is hung on three suspension arches, and the middle one had seventeen uprights. By any mathematics the ninth upright must be in the middle.

I reached it with two minutes to spare, turned my back on the bridge and leaned over the iron parapet.

A tug was fussing up stream, pulling a line of three barges. A pleasure steamer, its top deck almost empty, swung away from the landing stage, the band playing. Half a dozen clocks together started to chime the hour of nine.

Nothing else happened.

Looking out of the corner of my eye I totted up the score. An elderly German and his wife were walking towards me on the footway. They looked as ordinary as bread and butter. A small boy in leather shorts was coming the other way at a trot. A pair of blue uniformed bicyclists appeared from the Cathedral end and pedalled slowly towards me and past me. As they caught the gradient they put on speed a little, and disappeared.

It was nearly five past nine. A workman on a bicycle appeared at the west end. My instructions had been quite precise. It was beyond possibility that Henry should have made a mistake. I would stay until a quarter past nine and then try again next day. The workman jumped off his bicycle, propped it against the rail and leaned beside me. He had a small brown face like a friendly monkey.

"I take it you are Philip," he said.

"That's right." My German is adequate, but no more.

"Who did you get the message from?"

"Henry," I said, cautiously.

"All right, all right," he said. "No time for fencing. I'm sorry I'm late. I was damn nearly arrested this morning."

I expect I looked alarmed.

"Nothing to do with this business. Nothing at all. My own private life catching up with me. I'm doing this to oblige a friend. Every morning I come over on my way to work.

It's quite easy. When I saw that you were waiting for me, I stop."

"How did you know I was waiting for you?"

"How did I know? It was obvious. But never mind that." He glanced quickly over his shoulder, to left and right.

"You are to go to the Schloss Obersteinbruck. That is all I know. Now good-bye, and good luck."

"But where is it?"

"Above Steinbruck—as the name implies."

"And where is Steinbruck?"

"Good heavens," said the little man, "how should I know. Somewhere in Austria. You'll find it on the map."

He grabbed hold of his bicycle.

"Wait just a moment. When did you see Herr Studd-Thompson? Was he well? How long ago did he give you this message?"

"It was—let me see—two months. Perhaps more. Yes. he seemed very well."

"And you have come past here every morning for the last two months?"

"That is so. He did me a good turn, you see. A very good turn. Stolen goods, the police said. Of course it was a put up job. You understand?"

"I understand nothing—"

"That's right. That's quite right. Never understand a thing, then you can come to no harm. I must go now."

He hopped on to his bicycle and pedalled off. As he reached the far end a car drew out from where it had been waiting behind the buttress of the bridge. It quite blocked the footway.

I saw the bicycle wobble, then it straightened, and the rider hopped off. I thought for a moment he was going to run for it. But the two men who had got out of the car closed up on him.

I turned and walked fast in the other direction.

At the west end of the bridge another car was stationed. The driver was at the wheel; beside him another man with horn-rimmed glasses and a wide mouth like a fish.

Neither of them moved as I came up. I passed behind the

car, clattered down the steps, and walked off along the promenade. My heart was beating a little faster.

First I wanted to get off that promenade. It was too long and too straight and was commanded at both ends. Behind by the Hohenzollern Bridge which I had just left, and in front by the new Köln-Deutzer Bridge.

On my left I had been conscious of a looming white building. It turned out, when I got up to it, to be the Rhenisches-und-Historiches Museum. I bought a ticket off a snuffy old relic of the Franco-Prussian war and dived into shelter. Actually it was rather a nice museum, full of suits of armour, and engines of war and gigantic panoramas of the Rhine and a Vincenzo Coronelli globe from the Gymnasium Tricoronatum which, at any other time, I'd happily have spent the morning with. At that moment my mind was too occupied with the present to give due attention to the glories of the Rhenish past.

The rooms were almost empty. I sat myself down quietly on a seat behind a glass case of ladies' Sunday clothes, and listened. Ahead of me was the slow tip-tap of footsteps. They belonged to a little man who had come in just before me. In the silence I could follow his pottering progress from room to room. The only other sound was from the lobby where the custodian wheezed and coughed and occasionally rattled his cash box as if to assure himself that it was still with him.

Presently I heard the outer door open. Two more visitors. I sat tight, I was almost out of sight, but had a fair view of the room, between the sequin-covered bodices. This time it was two men, neither of whom I had seen before. They advanced steadily, wheeled to the right, and disappeared into the adjoining room. They didn't seem to be taking a great deal of interest in the history of the Rhine, either.

As soon as they were gone I got to my feet, blessing my rubber-soled shoes, and moved back the way I had come. The custodian seemed surprised to see me.

"It is forbidden to circulate in an against-the-clock direction," he said.

"An urgent appointment," I said firmly, vaulted the entrance turnstile, and trotted down the first steps. The custodian sat looking sourly after me. I had probably upset his calculations for the day.

Outside a police car was parked against the kerb. The driver looked worried when he saw me. His instructions had evidently not covered this contingency. I ignored him, and ran along the embankment. After all, it was no crime to run, even in Germany.

. The driver had an inspiration and started to sound his horn.

A stairway on the left. Just what I wanted. At the bottom an alleyway, and at the end of that another. Keep to the alleys. Cats can move in alleys. Cars can't.

There's a comfortably confusing network of alleys west of the Rhine at that point and it was a full quarter of a mile before I broke out into the Ringstrasse and immediately jumped on a tram.

I had no idea where it was going. The main point was that it was crowded, and moving. It made a swaying, jolting detour round most of the west suburbs of Cologne and finally dropped me at the Main Station.

The sweat was dry on me, and I was beginning to think. I went into the Station Buffet and bought myself a coffee. What had happened was now reasonably clear to me. The little man on the bridge had spoken the truth when he had said that his private life was catching up with him. It was catching up with *me* too. He was clearly a professional criminal. That the only reliable messenger in Cologne known to Colin should be a professional criminal was a piece of bad luck. That the police should have been planning to pull him in that morning was worse.

When they saw him stop and talk to me I became an object of suspicion too; and no wonder.

Were they still on my tail? It is easy to imagine you are being followed, but in this case I thought not. They would have had to be exceptionally quick and lucky to have picked me up as I came out of that maze of alleyways; and they would have needed a car at the exact spot to follow the tram.

Suppose for the moment I was all right. There were two flies in the ointment. The first was that I was too clearly a foreigner. The man in the car at the far end of the bridge had seen me closely enough to be sure about that. They may even have been able to identify me as an Englishman. The other thing was that I had a very healthy admiration for the German control of hotels. Registration was no mere formality, as it is in England. It was an efficient system designed to keep tabs on all strangers. It worked. I knew; I had had some before.

Regretfully I bade farewell to a suitcase full of new clothes, paid for my coffee, and made my way out. I knew just what I wanted. There is a large, new, department store on the Bendlerstrasse which specialises in men's clothes. Also it has dressing rooms.

When I came out in half an hour's time I was wearing (starting from the bottom) brogue flap-tongue shoes, white knitted stockings, cutaway leather shorts, a checked shirt, a bumfreezer jacket and a rather saucy Tyrolean hat with a synthetic badger's tail in the turned up brim.

My own clothes were neatly packed into the rucksack on my back. I carried a stick with a hartshorn handle.

I wondered for a moment if I had overdone it, but my fears were quickly dispelled. No one spared me a glance. The Germans, like the Americans, take kindly to fancy dress. Indeed, to wear a uniform of any sort is to classify yourself, and the Germans are keen on classification.

Organise yourself, organise your country, organise the world. Bless their orderly little hearts.

I bought a third class ticket for Baden which was in the right direction and seemed a logical place for a hiker to go to. I was in no particular hurry. It was Saturday. It was summer. The Continent was in front of me.

Late on Monday morning, after five more changes of train and two changes of clothes I saw Steinbruck for the first time.

We had left Graz at dawn. East of Volkermarkt the train pulls out of the plain and drags itself up for a few miles into the foothills. This small amount of extra height gave depth and meaning to the scene. From then on it was a journey of enchantment.

I studied the large scale map I had bought in Klagenfurt.

Steinbruck is an outpost. It sprawls between the foothills and the Raab, its frontage the river, its backcloth the magnificent semicircle of purple mountains which delimits the borders and meeting place of the ancient kingdoms of Hungary and Austria with the infant republic of Jugoslavia.

The mountains to the south had on their summer dress, laced along their lower slopes with the green vineyards.

But there was snow on the high tops and in the corries. As the train swung round a bend I was able to pick out the Klein-Oos and to follow its wandering course upwards. First through a cluster of red roofs which must mark the village of Kleinoosberg. Then up and up again, into the pine trees until—yes, there it was—topping the highest tree, built on to and into its pinnacle crag; the Schloss Obersteinbruck.

I could see what Colin meant when he told Henry it was a fairy palace. Without doubt Snow White had lived there. The Sleeping Beauty had lain in its tower-room and wolves still howled through the dark forest at its foot.

The train gave a derisive hoot, swung south again, and snorted down towards the town. I got out into the sunshine.

A long, straight avenue, bordered with plane trees, leads from the station to the town. Steinbruck is a relic from another age, an Edwardian-German spa, decayed but unchanged. There was the Kurhaus; there the mineral water fountain; there the tea garden. The covered stand for the orchestra. The concert room; the Tissichhaus and the Schlossgarten, their plaster flaking, their paint peeling, but still indomitably committed to the rigours of holiday-making.

I walked down a green allée towards the central square. One side of it was formed by the Casino. It did not look like a place where play would be high. More space would be given to family games of Dreizig-Vierzig than to baccarat. The pillars of the portico were cracked and along the front

stood orange trees in tubs. To the right the road runs up
the foothills; to the left, down to the river ("To the Island
of Pleasure" says a notice board. "Season tickets, or by the
day").

An air of solid, contented, melancholy sits on the place,
like a veil on the face of an elderly nun.

I went into the nearest Espresso and ordered coffee. It
took a long time to come. Nothing moves fast in Steinbruck.
I looked again at my map. The castle was three or four miles
from the town, and more than a thousand feet above it. I
sought out a garage and hired myself a car.

I have no recollection of the drive. My mind was ahead of
me. Would Colin be there? What was it all about? Why had
he stretched out this thread across Europe? It was a thin
thread, tenuous and easily broken, but a twitch on it had
been enough to bring me running.

We ground up the final ascent, and pulled to a stop, steam
jetting from our radiator, before an iron studded door let
into the living rock.

The driver hooted. A huge dog, lying in the sun, scratched
itself. The driver climbed out and pulled at a bell.

For a long time nothing happened. Then, quickly and
surprisingly quietly, the door opened. A tiny man, in some
sort of livery, peered politely out.

The moment had arrived.

I took a sealed envelope from my pocket—it contained the
original cutting from *The Times*—and handed it without a
word to the gnome.

He looked me quickly up and down, then said, in German
"Would you like to wait inside?"

I said yes to that, and paid off the car, which made a
shuddering turn and started coasting down the hill. I
reckoned he wouldn't have to use his engine until he got
back to the outskirts of the town.

I turned and followed my guide up a sloping cobbled
passage, and out into the courtyard at the end of it.

Chapter IV

LISA PRINZ AND MAJOR PIPER

FROM the inner courtyard the size of the place became more apparent. Colin had been accurate in his description. It was a palace, not a castle.

I am not good at buildings, but I shouldn't have said that it was much more than a hundred or maybe a hundred and fifty years old. Something older may very likely have been pulled down to make room for it. The fortress-like outer keep suggested a more ancient past. The inner portion looked like a hotel designed by an architect with illusions of grandeur.

I was shown into a small room on the left of the entrance portico, which might have been labelled "Reception". When the door opened, I think I half expected a hall porter in uniform.

Instead, it was Lisa!

"Phee-leep," she said. ('Said' is a most inadequate word. Lisa screams like a seagull when she is excited.) She came darting over and gave me a peck on the cheek.

Considering that it was thirteen years since I had set eyes on her she was very little changed. Somewhat sharper, a bit more angular, less ingenuous, more experienced, but the same darting eyes and wide mouth.

"This is a nice surprise," I said sincerely. "Were you expecting me?"

"The last man in the world."

"Lisa, be truthful."

"Quite, quite truthful. When August came and said to me, "There is a visitor—an Englishman, I think—I had no idea. It might have been Anthony Eden—it might have been General Montgomery—"

"What a let-down," I said. "When it was only me."

Lisa said: "Well, it was rather. But how nice that it should have been just you and no one else."

"Is Colin here?"

"Well—no."

Something cold settled on my heart.

"How long is it since you have seen him?"

"Would you like to come and talk to the boss?"

"In a minute. How long since you saw Colin?"

"Philip! Two minutes and you start to bully."

"I'm not bullying. But I've come a long way to meet him, and I want to know."

"Today it is Monday. Last Monday was a week ago. Then another week. Then four days before that."

"He was here a fortnight ago last Thursday, then?"

"That is right. A fortnight back from last Thursday. Come along now."

"Has anyone heard from him since he left?"

"I do not know. Perhaps. Lady will tell you."

"Lady?"

"Ferenc Lady. He is the leader here. Did you not know?"

"I know nothing," I said. "Absolutely nothing."

As we walked towards the door Lisa gave my hand a little squeeze. We climbed together the broad stairs which led from the hall to the first-floor landing. Facing us was a double door of carved, unpainted, lime wood. Lisa went in without knocking and I followed. It was a big ante-room. A young man with a pale face and sad eyes behind thick, horn-rimmed glasses, sat at a desk. He was snipping a paragraph from a newspaper and pasting it into a giant scrap book. A pile of mutilated paper lay on the floor behind him.

He looked politely at us.

"Gheorge," said Lisa. "This is Philip."

"Pleased to meet you, Mr. Philips."

"Well—actually Philip—"

"Mr. Philip."

I gave it up.

"This is Gheorge Ossudsky. He is Ferenc Lady's private secretary—and watch dog."

Gheorge said, seriously, "You over-rate my capabilities, Lisa. And why should Lady need a watch dog. He is well able to watch after himself."

" Is the great man busy?"

"I do not think so. Perhaps I will go in and ask."

"If you ask him, of course he'll say he's busy. Just announce Philip. Say that he has come from England with a message for him."

"Hey—" I said.

"That is all right. You want to talk to him, I suppose.'

"I suppose so," I said, weakly. Gheorge disappeared. There was a murmur of voices behind the partition. He reappeared and beckoned. Lisa gave my arm another little squeeze. I recognised it. It was just the sort of squeeze my mother used to give me before I walked into the dentist's surgery.

The inner room was small, but well proportioned. A drawing room in the scheme of things, I guessed; but the original furniture and carpets had been turned out and replaced by a desk, a conference table, and a number of chairs. On the the walls, where the pictures and tapestries had once hung, were maps—huge maps, in thick relief and in bold colour; the sort of maps which my mind associated with a military headquarters.

Ferenc Lady had got up from behind the desk as I came in. My first reaction was plain surprise; my next, something akin to dismay. It was the build-up that was to blame. I had been expecting a pocket Mussolini. What I saw was a small, petulant looking gentleman wearing one of the most terrible drape jackets I have ever seen off the West End stage. His small featured, sallow face would have been good-looking if he had not been so obviously irritated. I judged him to be as young or younger than me.

"Do I know you?"

He was, as I discovered afterwards, trilingual. On this

occasion he spoke in his native Hungarian. I answered him in the same tongue.

" I am afraid you do not. But the score is level, because until five minutes ago I had no idea you existed, either."

His teeth flashed in a smile of pure ill-humour.

"Perhaps you would like to sit down and tell me about yourself?"

As he jerked his head, a little waft of something-or-other-of violets reached me. I felt sure I was going to love him.

"When did you learn to speak Hungarian?"

"During the war. I spent a year in Hungary."

"A spy?"

"Certainly not. An escaping prisoner-of-war."

"You are not very fluent. Your vocal sounds are too thick and you use the English word order. A Hungarian would say "A year in Hungary I spent.""

"Would you prefer to talk in English?"

"As you like."

He switched smoothly into English. There was a touch of Belsize Park about it, but he was perfectly fluent and even colloquial.

"What brings you here?"

I told him about Colin Studd-Thompson and the advertisement. It didn't sound terribly convincing, but I've often found that's the way with the truth. It never sounds quite as reasonable as a good, logical, well-constructed lie.

Lady listened in silence. The only animation he showed was when I told him about my contact in Cologne getting picked up by the police. He made me describe the man again; then the details of his arrest.

"How did you know they were police?"

"All police look alike," I said. "It's a sort of beefy, stolid, holier-then-thou look. Once seen never forgotten."

"I think perhaps you jump to conclusions," he said. "Tell me again about Studd-Thompson. A childhood friendship, you say?"

"That's right. We used to cry each other to sleep, every night at school."

"Really," he said. "That sounds improbable."

I saw then, that it was no use trying to pull his leg. His skin was about two inches thick and satire-proof.

"And apart from this fortuitous friendship, you have no connection with our enterprise here?"

"I'm afraid I don't even know what your enterprise is," I confessed.

This confession seemed to cheer him up no end. He got up and walked round the room. The idea seemed to be that I should walk behind him, so I obliged.

"We are engaged," he said, "in ethnographical research. Speaking ethnographically, we stand here at the centre point of Europe. You follow the colour scheme." He pointed to the nearest map. "Dark blue is for the Germanic races. Light blue the Austro-Germans. Then we have the Magyars, the Slovaks and the Croats—each with its own subsidiary and mixed racial derivatives."

"I see," I said, untruthfully.

"You have made a study of these matters?"

"I know as much about ethnography as I know about making rice pudding."

"Ah. Then you'll excuse me asking this, I know. Why did Studd-Thompson want you to join us?"

"That," I said wearily, "is surely something that we can ask him, when he comes back from wherever he has gone."

Lady's lips moved gently. I could see he was repeating my last few words.

"When he comes back from wherever he has gone."

Then he said: "So you have no idea why he wanted you out here?"

"None at all."

"But you are old friends?"

"Our friendship started a long time ago."

"And he had never mentioned what he was doing here?"

"Possibly he realized that I was not interested in ethnography."

Lady allowed himself something which, in a less tightly

composed man, might have passed for a smile. A lifting of the upper lip.

"That would be it, I expect," he said. "Now, what are you going to do?"

"Wait for Colin."

"Here?"

I controlled myself.

"If you can't put me up," I said, "I have no doubt that I can find a room in one of the many hotels in Steinbruck. It looked a nice, cheerful, gossipy sort of place."

"No," he said. "I am afraid I couldn't allow you to stay in Steinbruck."

"How far away would you like me to go?"

"I think I should like you to go back to England."

"Well, think again."

The trouble was, I realised, that I was losing my temper, whilst he was not. The disadvantages of such a situation are obvious. I made the necessary effort.

"Let's be rational," I said. "I don't know what the set-up is here, but you can't turn me out of Steinbruck. I have a perfect right to be here. If I start asking questions round Steinbruck—"

The alarm was carefully concealed, but it was there. I had found a tender spot.

"On second thoughts," said Lady. "I think you had better stay here."

"I think that's one of the most gracious invitations I have ever received," I said. "I really can't refuse."

"Gheorge will allot you a room."

"That's all right," I said. "I've got a friend in the management."

Lady looked up sharply.

"Who?"

"A lady I had the good fortune to meet during the war."

"Lisa? Yes? Where?"

"As I told you. I was a prisoner of war. I escaped from Germany into Poland. Then from Poland across Czechoslovakia into Hungary. I was a year in Hungary—some of it in prison. Then I got out, and was helped into Jugoslavia. Lisa was one of the people who helped me."

"Interesting," said Lady. "She would have been at a romantic stage, of course."

"Of course," I agreed.

"You were friendly?"

"Oh, very friendly."

He just looked at me. It didn't matter to him. He wouldn't have minded if I'd murdered her old mother. It would have been a Factor; something to be discounted, or overcome, or perhaps just ignored.

"Then she will be a companion for you," he said, "until Studd-Thompson returns. You had better ask her to fix you up." As I turned to go he added: "There is one other thing. Here we are all of us guests. Our host is Baron Milo. We are free to do as we wish for the whole of the day, but he so far preserves the conventions of hospitality that he likes us to dine together at night. We meet at nine o'clock."

"I haven't got a dinner jacket."

"Gheorge is your size. He will lend you one."

"All right," I said, and made my escape.

Lisa was waiting for me.

"I have put your rucksack in your room," she said. "I will show you where it is. Is that all the clothes you have?"

"Every stitch," I said. "But I can soon buy some more."

"Have you got some money?"

"Lots of money."

"Good. There is a little man in Steinbruck will make you some clothes. It will take about two days."

"I wish I could introduce him to my tailor," I said. "He has never made me the simplest garment in less than two months. What about lunch?"

"We had better have that in the town. No one here eats much until the evening. Lady has some sandwiches sometimes when he is working very hard."

"You ought to have warned me."

"Of what?"

"He's a poisonous little man."

Lisa looked at me, cold astonishment in her eyes.

"But he is not poisonous," she said. "He is a great man."

"He couldn't be greater than he thinks he is."

"Philip, don't be so—" she cast round her diligently for the most wounding word in her vocabulary "so insular. Just because he does not behave in a hearty manner and slap you on the shoulder and say, "Old boy, old boy."

"If he had I should have assumed he was a confidence trickster."

"What's wrong with him then?"

"Nothing really," I said. "He dresses like a shopwalker and uses scent and has got an ego the size of a balloon—apart from that he's all right."

For a moment Lisa looked as if she was going to be angry. Then she laughed.

"Poor Phee-leep," she said. "You have always to be indignant about somebody. Yes? I remember. That is because you are a Martian."

"You still go in for that fiddle-faddle?"

"Because you do not understand it is no need to mock it."

My room was a nice one. I unpacked my rucksack, washed my face and put on my other collar. Whilst I was in the middle of these simple preparations there came a knock at the door and the gnome-like servitor came in. Thinking he had come to turn down the bed or something, I stood politely aside. But no. He had something to get off his chest. Having wound himself up, he pressed the button, and something came out which sounded like "affamissage".

"In case it's any help," I said, "I do speak Hungarian."

A broad smile split his oaken face.

"That is well," he said, with evident relief. "I have a message for you from your compatriot."

"From—?"

"From the Herr Studd-Thompson, yes. It is a message in writing."

"He left a letter?"

"Not for you, by name. He said to me, if I should go away, perhaps they will send someone in my stead. If it should be a little man, with brown skin and very light blue eyes and brown hair turning grey, then you will give him this letter."

I walked over to the glass. "Looks like me," I said.

The gnome grinned, and handed me an envelope. It had nothing written on it. I tore it open. Inside were two sheets of paper covered with Colin's neat, affected writing.

"I gather you got my first message, or you would hardly be reading this. I'm afraid I've been rather naughty, but you must put down some of it to boredom, and the rest to two interviews with that blazing ass Forestier. What I told him was that *if* anything should happen to prevent my playing my part in this business, then you were the best possible person to take my place. That's all. What he said to me was—(a) they couldn't possibly agree to my telling anyone anything about it (in the circumstances I can understand that) (b) that if someone else had to be roped in, it would be one of their own department, not you, and (c) if I made any attempt to communicate with you in any way, *I* should be for it, and *you* would be prevented from leaving England. That sounded to me like a threat. To which, assisted by my connections on *The Times*, by Henry (splendid woman) and by Herr Godinger of Cologne (provided he is still out of prison) I have devised, I venture to say, a fairly simple answer. Whether they will succeed in keeping you in England is a matter of opinion. My guess is no. Well, Philip, God bless you. I can't give you a more intelligent brief since I've no idea what I shall be doing, or what will be happening when this reaches you. Except that I shall be temporarily out of commission. Herewith I pass the torch to you."

I read it through twice. Then I became aware that the gnome was still with me.

"It is good news. Yes?"

"Yes," I said. "More or less."

"Not bad news?"

I gathered that he had become fond of Colin.

"Not bad," I said. "Certainly not bad."

Downstairs I found Lisa waiting for me impatiently.

We walked into Steinbruck together. Lisa, like a lot of upper class Hungarians, is a profound believer in Astrology. She herself favoured the "onamantic" method, which was tied up with numerology and seemed to me to be even more haphazard than the "scientific" method.

"I suppose you've worked out Lady's horoscope."

"But of course. He is a Jupiter. Loyalty, sincerity and inherent greatness."

"That seems to me sufficient proof that your system wants overhauling. What was I?"

"I told you. You are a Martian. Combative and quarrelsome. Also you are under the influence of Fish."

Before I could think of a suitable reply we were entering the town. Viewed as we came down into it from above, it looked larger than I had thought at first. A sprawling hotch potch of architecture. Streets of new buildings sprung up, like a fresh undergrowth, under the white towers and gables of the older Austrian buildings. It had all the charm of a town built on a slope between a mountain and a river. Some of the streets were mere flights of cobbled steps. It s air of settled but agreeable melancholy was even more remarkable at close quarters.

"They live in dreams," agreed Lisa. "Like Brighton."

We had our lunch in a restaurant overlooking the river. After two of my attempts to talk about Colin had been deftly turned aside I gave it up.

When we had finished our meal Lisa said: "I suppose now you will call on your representative."

" What representative?"

"Of your Government. I can show his office. You will wish to report yourself?"

"Why should I report to anyone," I said. "I'm not in the Army. I'm in Steinbruck as a tourist."

"We are rather far East for tourists," said Lisa. Her eyes had gone up as she spoke. From where we sat we could see the mountain edge, not very high, but sharp and defined, along which ran the last real barrier left in Europe.

"In any event," said Lisa, "if you do not go to see him he will hear of your arrival and will wonder. Major Piper is a very nice man. He will not eat you."

"I'm not afraid of him," I said. "If you think I ought to go, of course I will. Only, for various reasons, I think I'll not mention my real name."

"A new name. That's fun. What shall we christen you?"

I was devoid of inspiration.

"According to your natal sign, it should be Mr. Fish."

I drew the line at Fish. We compromised with Waters.

Major Piper had his office above a wine store. A faded board outside still showed the Sailing Ship which was the Corps Sign of the formation that had occupied Carinthia in 1945. Below it the letters A.M.G.O.T. had been painted out and 'H.M. Consular Agent' substituted; above it an arrow pointing down the passage. At the end of the passage a second arrow pointed us up the stairs.

The office of the local representative of H.M. Government was in two parts. In the outer part, at a table, sat a lady. Her hair was blonde, her proportions were generous, and she was asleep. Even in her sleep she managed to preserve a certain calm dignity.

We paused, irresolute.

Fortunately at that moment the old fashioned telephone at her desk rang.

She woke up and went into action without any appreciable intermission. I have seen cats wake like that, but never human beings.

"Hullo. Mitzi here. Yes." Then to us "Please sit down," and to the telephone "He is very busy now, could you possibly make it later?"

The telephone sounded irritated.

"But certainly he is busy," said the girl. "Poor man, he was up all last night." Here the telephone evidently made an unkind suggestion. Mitzi said: "Certainly not. He was working," and rang off sharply.

"I'm sorry he's busy," said Lisa. "Perhaps we had better come back later."

"Only busy to that pig," said Mitzi. "I will tell him. What name?"

"This is Mr. Waters—an Englishman."

"I deduced it from his clothes," said Mitzi, and disappeared into the inner office. The partition was thin and it was clear that she was now waking up Major Piper. Presently she beckoned us in.

The Major was a small, spare figure of a man. He could hardly, I thought, have been less than sixty. His flattened nose and broad, squashed face gave him the look of one of those peculiar Tasmanian mammals whose name I can never remember. His cheeks were rosy with interrupted sleep.

"Ah, hullo Lisa," he said. "Nice to see you. And you, Waters. We don't see many tourists here. Not enough attractions, you know."

"I have rarely seen a town I liked so much at first sight," I said, and meant it.

"Not really. You mean that? Well, I must say, I'm fond of it myself. I've been here ten years. A bit sleepy, perhaps. It wasn't like that when I first came here. I was in A.M.G.O.T. Plenty of life then."

"To tell you the truth," I said. "I hadn't realised that the Eastern boundary of our zone ever ran so far beyond Volkermarkt."

"I don't believe it was meant to be here," admitted the Major. "Result of a mistake—like the rest of the British Empire. I'm told it was a second Lieutenant in the 17/21st who couldn't read a map. No cavalry man ever can read a map. He was sent out to make contact with his Russian opposite number. Went to quite the wrong place. Finished up here. Of course, things were very fluid just at that time, with the Russos steamrollering in from Hungary, and the Jugs coming up from the South and the Eighth Army popping in from Italy three days ahead of schedule. Very off-putting for the politicians. Everything had to be decided on the spot in those days."

He sighed wistfully.

"You must be almost the furthest East of any neutral territory," I said.

"That's it," he said. "An outpost." The idea seemed to please him. "Of course, the real chap who matters here is the Soviet Trade Counsellor. Name of Palantrev. You won't meet him. No one ever does. For years I didn't believe he existed, and then one evening I ran across him at a cocktail party. Funny little man. Small, fat and frisky, like a biscuit-fed mouse."

"You say he's the real power," I said. "How's that? There aren't any Russian troops here."

"Not here," admitted the Major. "Not as far as I know. Plenty over the border, though. Line-of-communication troops they call them. They looked fairly operational to me the only time I saw them. Of course, they're not meant to be there at all. They were only supposed to be there whilst the occupation was on."

"Which no doubt accounts for the fact that they weren't in any hurry to sign a treaty with Austria."

"No doubt," he said, and looked at me sharply, as if I was the one who had been being indiscreet. "Where are you staying, Mr. Waters?"

"He's staying with us," said Lisa. "We'll see he doesn't get into any trouble."

"An ethnographer, eh?"

"Mr. Waters is one of the leading experts on the correlation of Slavonic and Teutonic racial characteristics."

"Ah, that accounts for it," said the Major. "I thought I recognised his name when you mentioned it. I've no doubt I'll run across you both from time to time."

We took our leave. Mitzi was boiling a large saucepan of chocolate on a gas ring in the outer office. She grinned at us.

"Might have offered us some," said Lisa. "It makes me slaver at the mouth just to look at it. Come to the Schloss-garten."

On the way to the Schlossgarten we dived down a close and up two flights of stairs to meet Lisa's tailor. He was a nice old man, who worked in a small room which seemed smaller because of the number of children in it. During the process of being measured I counted eight, but there may well have been more.

I ordered a dinner jacket, a suit for rough wear complete with knicker bockers ('le sporting') and a sober suit of dark grey with a generous roll to the lapels which is the uniform of all respectable continental racketeers.

Then we went to the Schlossgarten and drank our chocolate sitting under a striped umbrella with moth holes in it.

As we sat there the sun started to go down and a long shadow crept over the town from the west. The mountain line to the east was still warmed by the level sun but the shadows were stealing up the lower slopes.

Lisa followed my eyes.

"It's just like a fairy story," I said. "Not the nice, pretty, Walt Disney sort, but an old German fairy story with wood-cuts. Whilst the sun shines, girls and boys play. But when it starts to go down, and the long shadows begin to creep, all wise children go indoors and pull up the drawbridge, and the creatures of the night come out and play till cockcrow. The little wicked creatures who live in the trunks of trees, and the night birds who talk to each other in whispers, and worst of all, the men with fox faces. They look like men, and you can't be sure of them until they take off their shoes and stockings and you can see the hair between their toes."

Lisa said, "It is true. And in the morning, all the mountain line to the East is black and hard like the end of the known world. Then the sun comes up very slowly, and for a moment it turns everything red, like blood, before it comes flooding down into our valley, and life begins again."

She gave a little shiver.

"I should have brought my coat. Come on, we will walk up the hill and warm our blood. Also, we must not be late for dinner."

Gheorge's dinner jacket was a reasonable fit. He was longer in the arm than me but not quite so broad in the shoulders.

I walked into the drawing-room a few minutes before nine.

There were five people already there. I identified without difficulty the Frau Baronin, a tightly corseted old lady with the face and bearing of Senior Treasury Counsel; (she was deaf but apparently in possession of all her other faculties). The Baron Milo, a vital septuagenarian, was in front of the fire, with his son, General Milo, beside him. I had heard of the General. He had started the war in command of a Panzer Division, but his reputation as an intellectual had diverted him from commanding troops and looking after Districts to more confidential, and, in the outcome, more harmless fields of work. He had steered clear with equal skill of the Assasination Plot, and the War Crimes Trials and if he had had an ounce of military ambition he could have had a top job in the new German Army. Colin had often spoken of him and I looked at him with interest. He regarded me blankly in return through his heavy horn-rimmed spectacles.

Gheorge was talking earnestly to Lady (who had confirmed my worst suspicions by putting on a dinner jacket with dark green velvet facings); and at that moment Lisa came in.

"All here," announced the Baron, I could see him practically licking his lips. He jerked the bell beside the fireplace and a servant, who had evidently been waiting on the mark, swept open the inner doors and we passed, in an orderly rush, into the dining-room, Lady leading with the Frau Baronin, followed by the Baron and Lisa, Gheorge and myself, with the General whipping in.

Accounts of what other people eat are generally boring, so all I will say is that the food at this and every other meal I had at Schloss Obersteinbruck was perfect beyond modern understanding. I am a parsimonious eater at the best of times, and the bulk and succession of the dishes was a little daunting but nobody worried if you said 'No'. There was always something else to follow. I could understand how Colin had put on weight.

Until the very end of the meal we drank nothing but Tokay. Gheorge, who sat on my left, said "The Baron is a great lover of wine. He imports his Tokay himself from Hungary."

"And his girls from Yugoslavia," said Lisa, in what was

meant for a confidential aside, but fell embarrassingly into a gap in the conversation. Gheorge frowned at her.

After dinner we took our brandy with us into the drawing-room, where a card table had been set up.

"I am told you play bridge," said Lady.

"Why, yes," I said. I may have sounded a little surprised.

"Before you came," explained Lady, "we were in a quandary. Three of us here are extremely fond of the game." He indicated the General and Gheorge, who were both smiling.

Well, at last my usefulness was being appreciated.

The General spread the cards and we cut for partners. I found myself with Gheorge.

Bridge is a game that no one can really understand except its devotees, and they can live in it. Normally, perhaps, rather sombre and uninteresting characters, at the card table they come to life. During the magic hours when the game has them in thrall they attack and defend, plot and counter plot, use all the weapons of diplomacy and bluff, display their strengths and weaknesses, and lay bare their innermost souls. All in the deft handling of fifty-two pieces of pasteboard.

Gheorge was a sound player of a painstaking sort. General Milo was a scientist, pure and simple. But Lady had a touch of genius. He was neither to have nor to hold. After two rubbers I thought I had pinned him down to one particular deceptive play—only to find to my cost, during the third, that he had planted the idea with motives of his own. It occurred to me to wonder, for an uneasy moment, what stakes we were playing for, but the two following rubbers redressed the balance.

The sixth rubber was long and very evenly contested. Finally the cards came down decisively in my favour, and sweeping aside the proferred sacrifices of the enemy we rode through to six hearts and victory. I got to my feet feeling curiously stiff.

"Bed time?" said the General, regretfully. I nodded and looked at my watch, I thought for a moment it must have stopped. It showed five o'clock.

Walking over I drew open the heavy curtain. The window

looked out over the tops of the trees. Mist and shadows filled the valley, but light had come back into the upper sky.

I have a faint recollection of staggering to my room where I pitched into sleep; sleep bedevilled by dreams of wolf-men and witches, with the faces of Lady and Lisa Prinz, who played cards for stakes beyond my understanding.

Part II

THE MIDDLE GAME

" And pat, and pitter-pat ; too soft to feel
How cunningly the velvet pads conceal
Five cruel hooks of steel....."

                    Battle of the Beasts.

Chapter V

MAJOR MESSELEN

WHEN I woke it took me more than the usual two moments to remember where I was. My watch, which I had forgotten to wind, had stopped at half-past six.

I climbed out of bed, padded across to the window, and pulled at the cord which operated the long heavily lined curtains. They slid back and I stood for a moment held by the picture.

The mountains filled the eye; from the Eastern side, where they ran up low, kindly, covered in vineyard and olive grove, through a quarter circle to the wolf fangs, which stabbed the sky to the South.

The sun was so high that it could not have been short of midday. I dressed and ran down. The drawing-room and dining-room were empty. I walked through them, into a smaller drawing-room and so out, on to the broad stone balcony.

The Baron was perched on a wicker chair. He held in his hand a pair of field glasses which he lowered from his eyes when he heard me coming.

"You are already up?"

"I thought I should be the last," I said.

"More probably the first. Except for myself and Herr Lady no one rises here before afternoon. For myself it is no hardship to rise early. I have an interest in bird study."

The only sign of life in the landscape was a group of young girls who were beating out washing on the stones of one of the mountain streams.

The Baron smiled, "Charming, are they not," he said, and handed me the glasses. (They were, as I had guessed by their looks, a most efficient pair of high magnification.)

"Such shoulders and buttocks," said the Baron. "You would suppose them professional wrestlers. But interesting."

I agreed that they were interesting.

"It is a lovely view from here." The Baron elevated his glasses from the washer-girls and swept the mountain circle. "We are within four miles of the Jugoslav frontier here, did you know? And six of the Hungarian."

"Well sited," I agreed. "From an ethnographical point of view."

The Baron looked at me. The resemblance to the late Emperor Franz Joseph was quite remarkable.

"Hungary," he said, "is a dull country, justified by her wines. You appreciated the Tokay we drank yesterday?"

"Yes indeed."

"As Jugoslavia is by its girls. You noticed the one who served the Tokay?"

"I am afraid, Baron, that my mind was entirely on the wine."

"Then you must look at her tonight. Have you experience of Jugoslavian girls?"

I was saved the necessity of answering by the arrival of Lisa. The Baron creaked to his feet and bowed. Lisa gave him a kiss behind the ear.

"Would you care for coffee?" she said to me.

There was nothing I could have cared for more. Lisa said, "Pull that bell and someone will come. The service here is old fashioned, but it works eventually."

I jerked at a ten yard strip of tapestry on the left of the fireplace and a minute or two later the door opened and a girl came in.

"We should like coffee," I said in German.

"So should I," said the girl, in the same language.

At that I looked again, and felt myself blushing. She was young, with fair hair and a simple linen dress cut rather high across the throat.

Lisa was laughing maliciously.

"It is your 'jeune fille' appearance," she said. "People all mistake you for the skivvy, do they not?"

The girl performed a demure little musical comedy bob and said: "Is there anything I can do for Monsieur?" this time in French.

"Excuse my appalling gaffe," I said, following her into the same language (which I speak clumsily) "and ask Lisa to introduce us."

"Trüe Kethely," said Lisa. "This is Phee-leep. He has a surname too, but it is extremely English and I cannot pronounce it."

"Philippe," she said.

"Trude."

"Please, no. Trüe. It is two syllables, but there is no 'd'."

At this moment a lady with a grey moustache and beard came in with coffee, brioches, and, surprisingly, a plate of cold spiced sausage and gherkins. (I can only suppose that this was for ornament. I never saw anyone touch it during my stay at Obersteinbruck.) The coffee was excellent and my morale was so high that when Lady arrived I even managed to greet him with a cheerful good morning.

It was ignored.

He addressed himself to Trüe. "*When* you are ready," he said. "I have some letters for you to write." He banged out as abruptly as he had come. Trüe swallowed the remains of her coffee at a pace which brought tears to her eyes and scuttled after him.

"If I spoke to my secretary like that," I said, "or, indeed, to any typist in my office, she would first throw her typewriter at me and then remove herself, fast, to an employer with manners."

"It would be a mistake," said Lisa, seriously, "to judge us by English standards, Lady was born under the Twins. Like all Geminians he has two sides to his nature—"

"So far as I'm concerned," I said, "he can keep them both."

"Also he is worried this morning. There is something—I do not understand it. A man who was found in the river yesterday."

"A man?"

"A young man who worked in the Schneidermeister wine shop. He was courting one of the servants here. He would sometimes be up here, after dark.

"Schneidermeister," I said. The radar gave back a very faint echo. It is a common German surname, but I had seen it recently. Then I got it. It was the wine merchant who occupied the ground floor building where Major Piper had his office.

I asked Lisa.

"That is right," she said. "Kurt Schneidermeister is the wine merchant. He is a big man. Huge, I mean." She held her arms wide. "Like a tub. He is the most important wine merchant in this part of the country. The Baron knows him well."

"Yes," I said, disentangling it slowly as I went along. "But why should the fact that one of his men who also happened to be courting one of the castle maids, is now found drowned in the river be a source of worry to our lord and master?"

"You must not sneer," said Lisa. "It upsets the balance of your face."

I gave it up.

"Besides, I have something to tell you about Colin."

"Something—?"

"No," said Lisa. "I have heard nothing. But I have remembered something. There was one man in Steinbruck that Colin used to see more than any other. He is a German. His name is Messelen, Major Messelen. He was, I think, in Rommel's Army in Africa."

"And why should this character know where Colin is, if you and the authorities do not?"

"I did not say that he would know where Colin is. But he could tell you about him, perhaps, that is all. And do not snap."

"I didn't mean to snap," I said, and gave her a brotherly squeeze. "I'll talk to the whole Afrika Corps if there's a chance it'll help. Where does he live?"

She gave me the address. I could see that she was upset about something. Probably the truth was that when Lady was in one of his difficult moods everyone in the castle reacted. Except the Baron. He was back bird watching.

Number 40 (bis) Marienkirchestrasse was a dilapidated, whitewashed, many shuttered, steep roofed house in a close behind the church, let out in one and two roomed apartments.

On the second floor there was a choice of doors. I knocked at two without success, and tried the third, which gave onto the back of the house. There was life in that one. Someone was whistling.

I knocked again, then pressed on the door, which swung open. The whistling stopped, and a voice said, in the gemütlich Bavarian dialect: "Who is it? Come in, anyway."

The first impression I got was that the room was full of sunlight. Both big windows at the back were wide open, and the sun streamed in, gleaming from the brass wire of five or six birdcages. There was very little furniture in the room. A tiled stove, a few chairs, and a scrubbed table. Behind the table sat a man of about forty. He had light hair cut very short, light eyes, a short nose which started out in one direction and finished in another, and that sort of sandblasted skin and general appearance of having been smoothed off on an emery-wheel which will be forever associated with General Rommel. Even in shirt sleeves his late profession sat squarely on his shoulders.

"To what," he said, "does one owe what is commonly, but sometimes mistakenly, called the pleasure?"

"I'm sorry to intrude," I said, in my best German.

His face lit up.

"Another Englishman."

"Since you say 'another' there is a possibility that you knew a friend of mine. Herr Studd-Thompson."

"I know Mr. Thompson, yes. Mr. Colin—Studd-Thompson." He pronounced each word with relish. "A most friendly and agreeable character. A friend of yours, you say?"

"A very old friend. I have come here to find him."

"He has been lost, then?"

"That is where I hoped you might be able to help me."

"Alas, no. I have not seen Mr. Thompson for—oh—more than three weeks."

"But I understand that you used to see quite a lot of him?"

"That is true, Mr—?"

I told him my name, but without much hope. He tried it in three different ways and then gave it up. "Call me Philip," I said.

"Very well, Mr. Philip. Yes. I saw him often. We had interests which we shared. For instance—"

He moved to his feet with the sort of smoothness I should have expected from a man half his age, and opened a wall cupboard. Three of the shelves were piled with albums. He smoothed his fingers across them, pulled one out, and laid it on the table. "South American issues," he said. "Some of them very rare."

He pointed to one small green stamp which sat alone in its glory, in the centre of a blank page. "I had three thousand dollars offered to me for that one. I said no. It will soon be worth more."

I could make out that it was a picture of a small, fierce man with a pointed beard in a frame of snakes and monkeys. It didn't appeal to me as a thousand pounds worth of my money.

"I'm afraid I know nothing about them," I said.

"No? Your friend was knowledgeable."

That I could believe. The ever widening circle of Colin's knowledge could have embraced philately as easily as it had engulfed Esperanto.

"Were stamps the only thing you used to talk about?" I said.

The Major held his hand up. "A moment," he said.

Suddenly, near at hand, outside the window, the great clock of the Marienkirche began to speak for the hour. First came a triple four-note introduction. Then the great bell chimed twice. In the silence that followed I heard all the song birds trying to outsing their great brass rival. It was one of the most ludicrous but touching things I have ever heard.

"Absurd, is it not," said Messelen. "I had a cock bird who broke his heart trying to drown the big bell at midday. You were saying—"

I wasn't really saying anything. I was casting about wildly for a lead. "I was told you you knew Colin well. It had occurred to me to hope—"

"We had tastes in common," said Messelen. "That was all. We liked stamps and we enjoyed the pizzup."

"The—?"

He made the gesture of one lifting a tankard to his lips. Enlightenment came. "Well," I said. "I'm not what you'd call a violent drinker, but if you'd fancy a couple this evening I'd be very glad to join you."

"At the Pleasure Island, then, at eight o'clock."

I had a solitary lunch in the town, took the bus to Kleinoosberg and walked the rest of the way back to the castle. There was no one about so I went up to my room and went to sleep on my bed and woke up three hours later with a mouth full of wood shavings and a dear little baby headache.

It was in no very good temper that I sought out Lisa, and told her that I should not be in to dinner that evening."

"But you must be," she said. "We all attend dinner. The Baron will be most disappointed."

"He managed to get on very well without me until yesterday," I pointed out.

"Also you will spoil the bridge four. Lady will be furious."

"What did they do before I came? Play three handed nap?"

"I had to play, to make up the number."

"You have all my sympathy," I said. "If Lady isn't in a better temper than he was this morning I should prefer to be further away from him than the width of a bridge table."

I then went off and had a cold bath.

At eight o'clock exactly I entered Pleasure Island. It was a curious place; about an acre in extent and roughly the shape of an Aircraft Carrier. It had, apparently been laid out by a committee of discrepant tastes. It contained, in no particular sort of order, a beergarden, an aquarium, a reading room, an open air orchestra and stand, a swimming bath and a section labelled "Circus and Sideshows." I have no doubt that in the heyday of Steinbruck the whole Island blazed with lights and swarmed with pleasure seekers but at that particular moment retrenchment was the order of the day and only the beergarden was really in action.

Messelen had a beer ready for me; with a small schnapps as a chaser.

We put that down and I ordered another. The orchestra filed on to the stand and a tall thin conductor wandered on, and bowed to a scatter of applause. An old man put up No. 1 on the board and the orchestra embarked on an obscure but hearty overture.

I have not concealed the fact that I had liked Messelen at sight. After a couple of beers I found no reason to like him less. We talked about the war. Messelen held the detached, professional, views of most German officers I have met. He had been in Norway and Russia before he reached North Africa and it was evident that he knew what he was talking about.

"The desert was a soldier's dream," he said. "If the whole matter had been deliberately stage-managed by the Generals concerned they would not have chosen better. Imagine it. Sufficiently far from the Oberkommando and set down in a huge, open space, without a lot of pathetic civilians getting in the way."

. About Russia and Norway he seemed less inclined to talk.

I asked him what he was doing now.

"I exist," he said. "I am agent here for Kontour." I knew the name. They are a big firm that specialises in harvesting machinery. We had once approached them to subcontract for lawn mower blades but their terms were too stiff. We thrashed the agricultural machinery market pretty thoroughly. It is warm work thinking out technicalities in a foreign language and we put back quite a bit of beer between us.

The orchestra, I was rather surprised to see, had worked through to Item 10—an imitation of a thunderstorm in the

Harz Mountains. We must have been there longer than I thought. I looked at my watch and saw that it was already nearly eleven o'clock.

Messelen leaned forward and said something. It coincided with the best efforts of the tympanist and I lost it. He said it again.

"Where?" I said.

"In the corner. No, to the right of the bandstand. With the fat man. A blonde."

The place seemed full of fat men with blondes. Suddenly I saw her.

"The big blonde."

"The one drinking beer?"

"That's right."

"What about her?"

"Only that I once saw Herr Thompson here with her."

With a final crash the Orchestra achieved its consummation. The last peals of thunder died away across the mountain tops. The Nibelungen stabled their horses and hung their armour on the wall. In the comparative silence I tried to order my thoughts.

I said: "But that's Mitzi—Major Piper's secretary."

"That is so. Also she sleeps with him."

I said, "Last time I saw them they were sleeping apart," but it went over his head.

"And you say that Colin used to—"

"I do not say that he slept with her."

"No. But you say that he came here with her."

"Once. Maybe more often. I do not think it was a secret."

I agreed that coming to Pleasure Island together would be an odd way of keeping a secret. The place was now absolutely jampacked with people. The orchestra was strapping away its instruments into wicker and canvas containers, and loud-speakers had started to give out bouncy jazz from a South German station.

Once I had assimilated the idea that the fastidious Colin should be seen about in public with a girl like Mitzi, a possible explanation occurred to me. Whatever Colin was doing he was presumably, more or less, in liaison with Major Piper. Rather than hang around him and his office he might have preferred to keep contact through Mitzi.

A waiter squeezed his way through to us with two more beers. As I paid him Messelen said: "You see the man with her now."

"The surly character with a bow tie?"

"Yes. His name is Wachs."

"He can keep it."

"He is a bad hat. A racketeer."

"You have rackets here, too?"

"Of course," said Messelen. "Here above all."

"What sort of rackets?"

"Well—there is a lot of traffic, over the frontiers, you understand. Into Jugoslavia—and into Hungary."

"Across the impregnable Iron Curtain?"

"Of course the Russians know about it; and control most of it. It is as useful to them as to—anyone else."

"And Wachs is in it?"

"He is what you would call a minor character."

"Even so," I said, "it's damned odd that he should be hanging round with the secretary to the Allied Consular Representative. I think this calls for action."

Messelen looked up.

"What do you propose to do?"

"For a start," I said, "we could follow them when they leave here."

"I do not advise it."

"There's no need for you to come."

It is one of my peculiarities that even whilst I am doing something silly the other half of me is able to stand back and criticise. Like Alice, I can even get sarcastic at my own expense.

For instance, I could see now that I was partly drunk; that Messelen was not as drunk as I was (or had a better head); and that he seemed to be weighing up whether I was going to make a fool of myself, and, if so, whether he ought to cut adrift now or tag along and see that I didn't get into too much trouble.

"They're off," I said.

Mitzi and her escort were fighting their way through the crowd.

As he came past our table I took a good look at Wachs. He was a heavy man with that expression of fixed illtemper which derives either from the childhood repressions or permanent stomach troubles. He was pushing through the other drinkers with about as much finesse as a rhinoceros making his way through the crowd at a drinking pool.

And he was steering Mitzi ahead of him, more as a battering ram than a gesture of courtesy. He looked a thoroughly ugly customer.

I gave him ten yards and then followed. Messelen came along with me.

It was all right on the Island. There were plenty of people about. As soon as we got into Steinbruck it was different. One or two couples were strolling back into town, but they were at long intervals. Without Messelen I should either have lost my quarry or made my pursuit obvious in the first hundred yards. Messelen seemed to guess where they were making for, and his knowledge of the lay-out did the rest. We dived down a side street, turned up a long back alley which was full of shadows and smells, stumbled up it, turned again, and began to move, more carefully now, up a flight of flat, cobbled, steps. At the top we paused. Silence reigned. We peered out.

About ten yards up the road Wachs was standing, entwined with Mitzi. He was eating the back of her neck.

After a pause for digestion they moved on. We allowed them to turn the corner and sprinted after them. Since Messelen, too, was wearing rubber soles, we made very little noise.

It was when we reached the corner that I realised, for the first time, exactly where we were. We were looking at the Schneidermeister wine store, and above it were the offices of Major Piper.

The street was in complete darkness. Municipal lighting in Steinbruck had got no further than the main streets and squares. A black cavern, with a grey ceiling. I think the same thought was in both our minds; That Wachs and the insatiable Mitzi were tucked into one of the doorways having a second course. In which case to go along the street was to invite discovery.

I felt Messelen's hand on my arm; and then saw for myself. A light was moving in Major Piper's office. It looked like a torch. Then more light. Someone had turned on the desk light. A hand drew down the blind.

"Cool," said Messelen in my ear. "To use the office for love making whilst the boss is away."

We moved along the street until we were opposite the window. We could see nothing, not even a shadow on the blind.

"I don't believe it." I said.

"You think, perhaps, some funny business?"

"I'm damned sure of it," I said. "Why should they come all this way, at this time of night, for a little simple necking. She's presumably got a flat somewhere. So has he."

"What do you propose?"

The beer and the brandy were still in me.

"Let's knock them up, and see what transpires," I said.

"You and me and who else," said Messelen. "That Wachs—I told you—he's a nasty character."

"So am I."

"If you go in, you go alone."

But I was wrong. Neither of us went in.

Lights had appeared at the top of the street. Head lights. As the car turned the corner we were caught by their bright and impersonal gaze. As if embarrassed by sighting us the lights blinked and dipped, and then the car drew slowly up to stop beside us.

Major Piper looked out of the driving seat.

"Well," he said, "fancy finding you here. And how are you, Major?"

"I'm fine," said Messelen.

"Can I give you a lift anywhere?"

"Me," said Messelen. "I live two streets from here. I'm sure Philip would be pleased."

Major Piper had got out and he must have seen the light in his own office. There seemed to be nothing left for me to say except, "It's very good of you."

"Not at all," said Major Piper. "Not at all. Anything to oblige a compatriot."

F

Chapter VI

BARON MILO AND THE FRAU BARONIN

NEXT morning I woke late, feeling bad. I had a suspicion that I had not only drunk too much the night before, but that in some way I had made a fool of myself. However, before I could get into a complicated state about it, I went to sleep again, and didn't wake up this time until two o'clock in the afternoon.

Me, the Sleeping Beauty.

I got up, shaved, dressed, and wandered down. The place was as lively as a boarding school in holiday time.

I tugged on the bell rope and when the bearded lady appeared demanded black coffee. She seemed unsurprised. Schloss Obersteinbruck was the sort of place where black coffee was drunk at all hours, I suspect.

Afterwards I annexed a rug from my bed, retired to the woods behind the castle and slept some more.

I dreamed that I was playing water polo for England and came to the surface with a struggle to find my face being licked by a mastiff. Attached to the mastiff by a steel chain was Trüe. She was laughing at me.

"It was a shame to wake you," she said. "For you looked sweet in your sleep."

"All right. You needn't tell me. Mouth open, and dribbling lightly."

"Certainly not. You mouth was tightly compressed like a typical reticent Englishman."

"How did you find me here?"

"Lippi found you. He is an industrious tracker. We train him every day on offal."

"That makes it quite perfect," I said, sleepily. From where I lay she looked wonderful. She looked all right from almost any angle, but all the cameras in Hollywood would have

sung together like the morning stars for joy if they could have
caught her just at that moment, with one hand on the big
dog's head and the rays of the dying sun making gold out of
her hair.

"Trüe," I said. "How old are you?"

"What a funny question to ask. Why do you wish to
know?"

"I've no idea," I said. "It's just one of those things we
always ask girls when we meet them in England."

"Ah, yes. I know. In England, you have a law. You must
not rape any girl until she is sixteen."

"It's time you went home," I said.

When we got back Lisa met us in the hall. She gave us a
quick, sharp, look, under those dark eyebrows, and said to
Trüe: "We have been looking for you."

"You ought to have sent out Tutti to hunt for Lippi," I
said.

"What has happened, Lisa?" said Trüe.

"He has had to go to London. He caught the four o'clock
train to Klagenfurt. From there he can fly."

"Curiously urgent," I said. They both looked at me.
"The problems of ethnography, I mean," I explained.
"Klagenfurt today. London tomorrow. Has he mislaid a
valuable Croat, or stumbled on the missing Slovene link?"

Trüe laughed.

Lisa said, rather sharply, "I do not enquire where he goes
or why."

"That's the girl," I said. "You and the Light Brigade."
I went up to change for dinner.

Dinner that evening proved rather good fun. Everyone
was more themselves with Lady away. And when I realised
that, I realised a little of the grip he had on these people.
Trüe, of course, was only a child, but Lisa and Gheorge and
the General were considerable personalities in their own
right. Yet it was only when the sun went in that you could
see the lesser lights.

When the wine came round I remembered what the Baron
had told me and took a quick look at the young lady who was

serving it. And I saw what he meant. She had black hair, sloe-black eyes, clear skin and a pouting mouth; and everything else that God ever gave woman.

The Baron called her something or other. It sounded like "Dim-Wits". She walked away from me with a petulant waggle, picking up a fairly hot glance from the Baron as she went by.

"Jugoslav," said Lisa in my ear.

"If I was Tito," I said, "I should put her on a list of forbidden exports."

"I don't think she came through the customs."

I was still digesting this thought when the party broke up. Trüe said something about filing and disappeared, like a good girl, who works even when the Boss isn't there, in the direction of the headquarters office. Gheorge Ossudsky went with her. The rest of us took our coffee into the small drawing-room.

(The more I saw of Schloss Obersteinbruck the more did Colin's description seem just. It was a most peculiar sort of fairy palace. It came to life at dusk. Then lights were kindled; fires sprang up in the grates; servants appeared who had not even existed before. From then until dawn the whole place hummed with suppressed, self-satisfied, life.)

"I understand," said the Baron, in careful English, "that all your great houses have now been turned into museums."

"A lot of them have," I said. "Some of the best of them are used as schools for delinquent children."

The Baron then translated his own observation and my comment to the Baronin, who gave out a sharp cackle. The conversation continued in this way for some time until the Baronin dropped off to sleep. The Baron then refilled my glass, and his own, with brandy and said, in a somewhat challenging voice: "You noticed Dmwitza then?"

"The young lady who handed round the Tokay?"

"The maid servant."

"Yes. I noticed her."

"What was your reaction to her?"

"A striking girl," I said.

"The girls of Northern Jugoslavia," said the Baron, speaking in the dispassionate voice proper to an ethnographer, "are constructed for love. They are all of the same mould. It is depth of body, you understand, that gives pleasure to love. They are as deep in body as—as they are shallow in wit. They have only one fault, to my mind. They are quite insatiable."

"Who are quite insatiable?" demanded the Baronin, waking up sharply.

"We were discussing the English Income Tax system, my dear."

"Ah, the English Income Tax system," said the Baronin. "In Austria we have the best system. We have no income tax." She disposed herself for sleep again, but the interruption had thrown the Baron out of his stride. He turned to politics.

"Here we are well placed," he said, "to watch the Soviet System in operation. We have, you might say, a dress cricle view of one of her most unmanageable satellites. Hungary."

"According to the newspapers, they seem to stage a purge or a re-shuffle every six months. I fancied, however, that they had been a little more stable recently."

"For the last year, yes. That is David Szormeny. He is a strong man. Too strong, perhaps. There is danger, you understand, in inserting a steel component into a machine which is otherwise constructed entirely of soft iron."

I tried to summon up my recollection of Szormeny. A few photographs had been allowed to filter across to the Western world. I remembered one of him at a Farm Worker's Congress. A tall man with an ugly, superficially pleasant face who reminded me of someone—I couldn't place it—one of our own public characters, perhaps.

"Since the war," said the Baron, "the fate of the popular leaders of Hungary has not been encouraging, you will agree. You remember Rakosi."

"Who died in a sanatorium in Moscow."

"Regretted," said the Baron. "Deeply regretted. He was given a Senior Hero's funeral with a procession exactly a mile long. Then there was Szakasits—he is still working out a comparatively lenient sentence of twenty years hard labour. And Laslo Rajk. Well, possibly he was the most fortunate They hanged him after a public trial."

"They were only puppets," I said. "The real leader was the Communist Secretary."

"Until last year, yes. But Szormeny *is* Secretary General of the Communist Party. As well as President of the Republic."

"Quite a boy," I said. "But I expect they'll execute him, for all that, next time the harvest fails."

The Baron elected to take this suggestion seriously.

"Not the harvest," he said. "In Bulgaria, yes. The Bulgars live like animals, by the soil. They know no better. But Hungary is an industrial country. They have skilled workers, and the workers have their own leaders. They were all Socialists until the Socialist Party was abolished."

"How easy you make it sound," I said. " 'The Socialist Party was abolished.' Just like that. Do you know there are people in England who would give their right hand to learn the trick."

"To abolish a workers' party does not entirely solve the problem of the workers," said the Baron. "There were Unions; a relic of 1944. These too, were abolished or absorbed. But it did not terminate the resistance. If a hundred thousand workers decide to work badly, you would need a hundred thousand overseers to prevent it. A Peyer can be imprisoned and a Kellemen executed but that will not make a single mechanic turn a screw or drive a rivet faster then he wishes."

"I see," I said, thoughtfully. "And is there much unrest?"

"There was," said the Baron, "until Szormeny doubled the industrial workers' ration and gave them certain privileges. Now they are quiet again."

At this point, to my annoyance, the Baronin fell out of her chair, and when we had picked her up and sorted her out the Baron decided that he had better take her off to bed.

Lisa had gone off to join Trüe and Gheorge in the office and I had decided to make for my own room and the prospect of an early bed when a cough from the deep armchair beside the fire reminded me that I was not, after all, alone.

It occurred to me that General Milo had somewhere acquired the art of sitting still. Now his head turned slowly and as his great glasses swivelled in my direction I felt like an enemy aeroplane caught by twin searchlights.

"I fear," he said, "that my father rides his hobby horse. You must stop him if you are bored."

"On the contrary," I said, sincerely. "I find him most interesting. And he seems, if I may say so, well informed."

The General turned this one over in his mind for a few seconds and then said, with all the deliberation of a chess player offering a gambit, "So he should be well informed."

I moved a pawn forward myself, and said "Why?"

The General did not answer this directly. He nodded his head at an oil painting above the fire. I saw it was Honneger's 'Duelling Students'. "My father lives in the past. He was at Heidelberg, you know. He still absurdly proud of a scar down the side of his chin. It was long a matter of anxious debate with him whether he should cultivate those Franz Joseph side whiskers. They suit him admirably, but they hide the scar."

I moved another pawn.

"Not a man who would take kindly to the restrictions of the modern world?"

" Far from it. He has been, you know, a great smuggler."

The outline became clearer.

"He is well placed for it here," I agreed. "I suppose he gets his Tokay from Hungary, and his girls from Jugoslavia. And pays no duty on either of them."

The General frowned very slightly. "You put the matter somewhat crudely," he said. "You will remember that my father is nearly eighty."

"I meant no disrespect. We could do with more individualists in our world today."

"Well," said the General. "That may be so. I will wish you good night."

I was unable to detect whether he was really annoyed with

me or not. A face trained in the fleshing sheds of Nazi politics was unlikely to give away much to a stranger.

It was after breakfast next morning that I happened to stroll along the terrace and turn into the long, dim conservatory which hung along the south wall of the Schloss.

The smell of any glasshouse, the wet earth and the greenery and the central heating, takes me straight back to my youth. Sunday morning, between my father and the head gardener, tremulously picking a flower for my mother.

"Nip it with your nails, Master Philip," and, "Long stalk, Philip," from my father.

This one was narrow and dim and full of hanging baskets of feathery Cycas and Cyathea. As I picked my way along the duck boards on the floor I realized that it was more extensive than I had thought, opening out finally into a balloon-shaped annexe at the corner. I also realised that the General had sadly underestimated his father's prowess. One of the long wicker chairs was occupied by the Baron. Another pulled up alongside it, by little Dim-Wits. He seemed to be engaged in tickling the front of her bodice with a palm frond. How she was reacting to this I was unable to observe as she had her back to me.

Blessing once more my rubber-soled shoes, I withdrew carefully, the way I had come. I was almost back at the terrace when a complication presented itself. The door clicked open, and the Baronin appeared.

She was moving slowly, but with the steady inevitability of a snail in a salad border; and I didn't really see how the Baron was going to get out of this one. He might of course, follow the example of the Duke of Marlborough and jump for it. But not only was he rather older than Churchill; he had about ten times as far to fall.

I backed nervously ahead of the Baronin. "A lovely collection you have here," I said.

"August keeps it quite ten degrees too hot," she said. I gathered after a moment's thought, that August was the head gardener, not the month.

"It is excellent for palms and ferns." She prodded a dark

green Cycas with her ivory headed, rubber tipped, stick. "But the seedlings grow too fast. Then, when they are potted out, they die."

I backed a bit further and resisted the impulse to look over my shoulder.

"Do you grow orchids," I said, loudly.

"My husband is very fond of them," agreed the Baronin. "He has a weakness for tropical flowers."

There was an element of Aldwych farce about the situation; but I found little inclination to laugh. The Baronin might be deafish but she was not blind nor, I felt certain, complaisant.

"You get a lovely view from here," I said, desperately.

This held her for a moment.

"On a clear day," she said, "you can see the tip of the Radkersberg."

"Would that be north or south of the pass?"

I indicated the white road which snaked up through the vineyards and disappeared round a shoulder of the mountain. (I assumed that the frontier post was on the other side. I could see no sign of it). Like most women she had little idea of topography. By the time we had fixed the relative positions of the pass and the Radkersberg I had got my second wind.

"Surely," I said, pointing over her shoulders the way we had come, "that is a flammarium orchid. I had no idea they could be grown in Europe—"

Once she had started in the other direction it wasn't so bad. It took ten minutes, and three more leading questions, to get her out on to the terrace, and after that, feeling that I couldn't very well drop her, I went with her to examine her collection of Japanese pot-pourri bowls.

That afternoon I went for a proper walk. I felt the need of it. Some people walk to keep fit, or to pass the time, or to work up an appetite. It doesn't take me that way. I walk for the sake of walking. After half an hour, at a stiff pace, some centrifugal armature flies back, some valve opens almost with an audible click and I find myself in concert and ticking over again. It is immaterial to me where I go. On this occasion I made my way down to Steinbruck, skirted the town to the left, went fast along the good road to Graz for about eight kilometres, then took the first track to the left. There was no chance of losing my way. The mountain crests to the south were ruled, in one dark, hard line, across the whole of my horizon. I was out for walking, not climbing, so I stopped when the track ran out of the forest on to the outcrop and swung east skirting the edge of the trees. The tops above me looked stiff, but nowhere unclimbable.

I kept up a fair pace, in and out of the gullies, and was back above Obersteinbruck by four o'clock. When the gnome answered the bell he told me the Baron wanted me. I asked if it was urgent. The gnome thought not. I had a bath, changed, and made my way to the Baron's study.

When I came in he got up, moved across and shook me by the hand. Nothing more was said, then or at any other time, about the incidents of the morning; but I reckoned I had received the accolade.

The Baron said, "By the way, I have news for you."

"News?"

"Of a friend of yours."

"Colin?"

" I would say also, a friend of mine. A most estimable young man. His knowledge of the intricacies of Hapsburg genealogy—quite remarkable."

"What have you heard?"

"It is, I fear, only at second-hand. But it may offer you a lead. I have, you know, friends in the—" The Baron paused for an instant—"the transport business."

"The General told me that you had interests in some of the neighbouring countries."

"That is so. Interests in neighbouring countries. There is a man in Steinbruck who does much work for me. Herr Schneidermeister—"

"I know him," I said. "A wine merchant, and shaped like a tub."

"So. He is a largely built man. But his sons are young and

active. They travel the countryside. They have not, perhaps, an undue respect for the artificial demarcations of frontiers—"

At any other time I should have enjoyed the courteous circumlocutions in which the Baron wrapped up the fact that he was hand in glove with a gang of smugglers. At the moment, however, I was too anxious to play.

"Tell me, please, Herr Baron," I said. "Who has seen Colin and where?"

"It was young Franz Schneidermeister. He was talking to a man called Thugutt, a Jugoslav of German origin, quite an ethnological curiosity himself—"

The Baron must have seen my face, because he hurried on. "He is a forester. A very useful man, who lives with his family on the Jugoslav side of the Austrian frontier line, in the mountains, overlooking Hungary."

I could well imagine that a man so placed would be useful to the Baron.

"And he had seen Colin?"

"I understand so. Either seen him or spoken to someone who has seen him. It was not easy to discover which, because on this occasion Thugutt appeared unanxious to talk. In fact, he would say very little. It seemed to Franz, however, that he might have talked, perhaps, if face to face with a personal friend of Studd-Thompson."

"Would he talk to me?"

"That was in my mind."

" When do I start?"

The Baron said, "On that we must consult Herr Lady."

"What's it got to do with him?"

"You must realise that we must not do anything to upset his plans."

"I could judge better of that if I had the least idea what his plans are."

"He has not told you, then?"

"I've been given a lot of cock and bull about ethnography which I not only didn't believe but I don't even think I was expected to believe."

"He will tell you in due course, I am sure."

"I'm afraid I can't wait," I said. "If you won't help me, I shall have to see Schneidermeister and do what I can on my own."

The Baron looked distressed. "I beg you," he said, "to wait for Herr Lady."

"Until he has finished buying his hand-sewn shirts or getting his hair cut in Bond Street, or whatever he has waltzed off to London for?"

An unaffected laugh brought my head round. Lady was inside the door.

"In fact," he said. "I *did* have time for a haircut at Mr. Truefitt's establishment, but, as you see, I have not allowed it to delay my return."

I said, truculently, "I don't know how long you've been eavesdropping, but if you heard what I told the Baron, you know what I want—"

"I expect it is the same as we all want. Would you be good enough to come with me?"

I followed him into the operations room. Lisa and Trüe were there, doing something to the maps. He waggled his little finger at them and they disappeared.

Then he looked up at me, and said: "You were the chief reason for my visit to London."

"Oh," I said, rather blankly. It was obvious enough, but it had not occurred to me. "What did they tell you?"

"Very little, except that you really were what you said. An old friend of Colin Studd-Thompson."

"Why should I have lied about it?"

"No reason why. No reason why not." He moulded the tip of a fresh cigarette between his thin brown fingers and added: "Also that, judging from your movements at the end of last week, you were a man of some resource. And that so far as they knew anything at all about you, of integrity."

"That only means," I said, "that they don't keep my papers in a buff file with a red label in the top left-hand corner."

"Quite so. As I said, they know nothing against you, and

very little about you. In the circumstances"—having got
the cigarette to his liking he squeezed it into his long amber
holder—"they have left the matter to my discretion. And I
have come to the conclusion that you should stay here, and
help us."

"Why?"

"Because I like you," said Lady, with a broad smile,
that might have meant anything. "And trust you, of course,"
he added.

"In other words, I'm here, and it might cause more trouble
if you tried to sling me out, than if you let me stay. And
anyway, whilst I'm here, you can keep an eye on me."

"My dear fellow," said Lady. "You insist on imputing
the worst of motives to everyone. It is a defect in your character. If I am to be candid with you, you must be candid
with me."

He sounded exactly like my housemaster.

"All right," I said. "Then you can be candid first. What's
it all about and you can leave out the ethnography."

Lady said: "Very well. You shall know."

And he told me. I won't try to reproduce it word for word
as he said it, because he took some time telling the story,
and I can't remember all of his background stuff. But what
it amounted to was this. The Western powers—America and
England specifically—had established a series of teams to
deal with the problems of each of the satellites. The "Equipe
Lady" were the top Hungarian specialists. It was quite a
large affair, with an office in the Hague and branches in
London and New York. Analysing the press reports and
monitoring the wireless were its bread-and-butter activities.
But there were more specialised branches. One of these was
concerned with screening all refugees from Hungary;
screening them and, in very exceptional circumstances,
sending them back again.

"We are not a military organisation," said Lady—and
looking him over, from his openwork shoes, via his shot-
silk shirt to his amber cigarette holder, I was forced to
agree that he did not fit into my picture of any military

headquarters. "Our rôle is to accumulate information. The larger part of it we get by sitting still and keeping out ears to the ground. Very occasionally, when there is an unexplained corner to be filled in, or some little job to be done, a man goes over the mountains."

"But here at Schloss Obersteinbruck," I said, "you are far from your comfortable offices in the Hague. In fact, you are at action stations. Why? Is a man being sent over the mountains?"

Lady looked at me. "I can perceive," he said, "why you were unpopular with your own Intelligence."

"But I want to know."

"Yes, a man went over the mountains."

"Colin?"

Lady's laugh sounded spontaneous. "Of course not," he said. "Why should we send an Englishman, who would be known every time he opened his mouth when we have a dozen home-grown Hungarians with families and backgrounds."

"All right," I said. "Then what was Colin doing here?"

"He was our liaison."

"With whom?"

"With our sponsors, of course. With England, and, through England with America."

That seemed possible enough.

I said, "I am sorry to ask so many questions. I know enough about Intelligence to realise that it is exceedingly bad form. The preferred attitude is one of studied indifference. But whilst you're in the mood there is one more thing I must know. What has happened to Colin?"

"He disappeared," said Lady, "three weeks ago. He walked down to Steinbruck one evening, and did not return."

"Who saw him last, and where?"

"He was at Pleasure Island, with Trüe—Miss Kethely."

"Yes, I know her."

"According to her, he made an excuse to leave her, pushed off into the crowd, and did not come back."

"No one else saw him?"

"No doubt other people saw him. But no one has come forward to say so—yet."

"And you have done nothing about it?"

"We have done what we could. One of our best local men was put on to the job."

"Yes," I said, bitterly. "And in a few months time he will report in triplicate to the effect that he has left no stone unturned and no avenue unexplored."

"He will not report to anyone," said Lady. "He was picked out of the river three days ago, a mile below the town. It is not clear whether he died by drowning or not. The top of his head was missing."

I cannot remember what else was said. Lady did not appear at dinner, which was a silent meal, and after it I went up early to my room. I undressed, turned the light out and sat for a long time in a chair in front of the window. I may even have dozed, for I have no idea what time it was when I opened my eyes and saw Trüe.

There was a clear, silver moon, quite full and undimmed by the faintest mist. Trüe had come out of the shrubbery at the foot of the long lawn. She looked like Titania in a belted raincoat. She walked slowly across the grass and I saw that there was no spring in her step. She had come either far or fast. I knew that she must be making for the little side door under the balcony; and that from there three flights of the back stairs would bring her out, into the passage, a few paces from my bedroom.

On an impulse I got to my feet, opened my own door, and stepped out into the carpeted passage.

It was only a minute before I heard her coming. If it had been longer my internal monitor would have told me I was behaving like a fool, and would have sent me back to bed. Dragging feet scuffled the stair carpet. As she came past I put a hand out and touched her am. She came round like a steel spring. Her hand went down, and up again, and a thin point, blue in the moonlight, touched my pyjama jacket.

If you should be so unwise as to touch a sleeping scorpion,

just so, on the touch, without the least intermission of time between sleeping and waking, the armoured tail swings round and is fastened to your finger.

Trüe dropped her hand and said, rather breathlessly. "Philip. That was a silly thing to do." Then she was gone.

I stood, watching her, a tiny cold feeling still tingling on my skin like a drop of iced water. Up the passage a door opened. There was a whisper of voices. A door shut.

Christ's sake, the place was like a rabbit warren.

Chapter VII

A JOURNEY IN THE PAST

I woke up thinking about Trüe. That was a warning, if I needed one.

I didn't see her until the afternoon, and by the time she came down I saw that twelve hours sleep had performed its customary service. Her eyes were clear and the spring was back in her step.

"Come out into the garden," she said, "and I will apologise."

"For what?"

"For last night. If I had not been frightened and tired I would not have done it."

"I'd like to see you perform when you're fresh," I said. "My navel is still tingling."

"I am adept with a knife," admitted Trüe. She spoke it in just the casual, self-deprecating way that an English girl might say, "I'm not bad at tennis, really."

"Let us sit in this summer-house," I said. "It is designed for confidences. You tell me the story of your life and I'll tell you mine. And stop Tutti from breathing in my face."

"Is he not a monster?" She said something in colloquial Hungarian to the mastiff, who removed himself from my chest, grumbled unhappily, and laid himself down across the opening of the summer-house like a sunken tree across a dam.

"I was born," she said "in Gyor."

"Of poor but honest parents."

"Not at all. They were very rich. We had a summer-house on Lake Balaton, and a town house in the Margit Korut in Buda."

"Next to the prison."

"Opposite. Why?"

"It's not my turn yet. Go on. What was your father?"

"He had estates."

"But what did he do?"

"Why should he do anything? He had the estates, you see. His people worked. He spent the money. He had a big collection of gramophone records. He said there was a man in America who had more than him, but I could not believe it. He had two whole rooms, quite full."

"And he spent his working life playing them."

"Now you are making fun of us. Of course he did other things. In the season we went to the opera almost every night. And in summer we lived at Badacsony on the lake, bathing and boating and—oh, having fun."

"It sounds lovely. Why did you stop?"

"First the Germans came. That was in 1944—just before Holy Week. They were very correct, but we did not like to stay in Buda. Besides, there might have been rationing."

"That, of course, would have been unspeakable. What did you do?"

"We went back to Badacsony. For that summer and autumn it was all right. Except the refugees, at the end, who came and ate up our food when there was not enough for us."

"And then?"

"Then the Russians came."

"They were not correct?"

Trüe looked at me to see whether I was joking. Then she laughed herself. But all in all it was not a convincing performance.

"Did your family escape?"

"No. They stayed too long."

"Do you know what happened to them?"

"Of course I know, they are dead."

(What a silly question! When the sea comes up either you get away or you are drowned.)

"I had been sent to Sopron with Anna, one of our old servants. She came from Austria, and her plan was to get back there. That was why we chose Sopron. It was close to the frontier. I cannot remember a great deal about that.

It was just before Christmas and we went in a train and it was very, very crowded, and very, very cold. We were in the carriage and we kept warm somehow because we were so many, but people who could not get in, stood on the foot-boards outside and some of them dropped off. In the end we came to Graz, where Anna lived, and we stayed there."

"What did you do?"

"I went back to school, of course, and learned History and Geography. Now that is enough about me. Tell me about you."

"Like you," I said, "I come of rich and dishonest parents. The only difference is that in England we make our rich men work. My father worked very hard indeed. He still does. It brought him a certain amount of public honour. When I grew up he wanted me to go into politics."

"Politics? That is defilement."

"I entirely agree," I said. "I can only say that it used to be thought to be all right. I'm afraid my father didn't realise quite how times had changed. So I decided for him that I would go in for the Law and I was called to the Bar. Since I found no work at all I had plenty of time to indulge in my hobbies."

"Which are?"

"Rock climbing and girls. You would be surprised how complementary the two pursuits are."

"I do not wish," said Trüe, with dignity, "to hear about your sexual conquests."

"I can assure you that I had no intention of mentioning them. I was going to talk about peaks I had climbed."

"Be serious, and talk to me about the war. You had adventures in the war."

"How do you happen to know that?"

"Lisa told me. And so did Colin."

"Well," I said. "It's a long story—"

So it was. The odd, sealed, chapter in my life. It had started on one Christmas day and ended on another, and had lasted exactly three years.

I was a 'Calais' prisoner and by Christmas 1940 I was, I

suppose, as happy as any prisoner of the Reich. My selfish, self-sufficient, temperament found a lot of satisfaction in the life of a prisoner of war. You don't need me to explain it to you. It's all in the books.

On that particular day I got drunk and decided to make a speech. I was helped on to the canteen table and spoke my mind for five minutes. It went well. I made the speech again, in Hungarian. This was an indiscretion. Finally, I delivered it in German.

The next morning before I had begun to recover from my hangover, I was on my way to Bolen, in Poland.

Bolen was not a pleasant place; I shared a room with the only other two English-speaking prisoners in the place; a tall mad, Flight-Lieutenant who circled endlessly in his Spitfire over Berlin, picking off prominent Nazi personalities; and a South African, whom I suspected of being a stool-pigeon, though what quarry he hoped to trap in that miserable, damp, snowswept, God-forgotten corner of the Eastern Reich it is beyond my imagination to conceive.

My only friend was a Pole, a brave and delightful seventeen year old boy called Karol. With Karol I climbed out of the camp, in the spring of 1941, and walked right through to his home, a farm in Southern Poland, near Wadowice. Here the desire to escape died on me; and I spent a very happy five or six months working in the fields by day and, in the evenings talking to Karol and his family, in my rapidly improving Polish. Long talks, in which we rebuilt the world for our pleasure. They were, I think, the nicest family I had ever known.

I passed as one Stefan, a distant cousin, from Warsaw. This was all right for a time, and I even got some sort of identity documents out of the local authorities. The trouble, as usual, started with neighbours; and specifically, I think, but have no sort of proof, with a girl who had made a proposal to me which I had rejected; more out of fastidiousness than lack of appetite.

I was suddenly bundled into a cabin in the woods with a week's food and told to lie low. I lay up, safe but badly troubled, for a week, and then crept back at dusk, to the farmhouse. It had been burned out, and the farmer, his wife and Karol nailed up outside it like jackdaws on a keeper's wall. There was nothing I could do about it. I set out, through the forest, for Czechoslavakia.

It was late summer, and because I did not, at that moment, greatly care whether I lived or died, I made that crossing safely and on my own. It was considered at that time, by refugees and lawless folk, to be one of the most closely guarded frontiers in Europe. There was, of course, an active Czech underground. But because the spectres of Karol and his family still walked behind my shoulder I refused to attach myself for long to any group or family. This may also have ministered to my safety. Resistance workers, like game birds, are easier to shoot if they will sit still. I could not now make out for you any sort of itinerary, but through that autumn I lived in a dozen different towns and cities and stayed with half a hundred people; people who have run together, in my mind, and faded into one composite blur. When a whole country is in opposition, when the active resisters are tens of thousands, they acquire a recognisable personality, fanatical, humourless, reliable, cold, twisted. Living amongst them I reached a stage where I could recognise a resistance worker in the street; could smell one in the dark.

I passed now for a Danziger. My Polish was quite good enough for this. A very few people knew who I was; enough to save me from getting my throat cut if a real Danziger had turned up to denounce me.

Although my moves were zig-zag and haphazard, I found myself drifting to the south; and by November I was ready for my next move, which was into Hungary. It was a trip which took a lot of arranging, and in the end three of us set out, too late, and ran into snow conditions in the South Tatra Mountains that we were not equipped to deal with. The route we chose would have been easy enough for a well equipped team but we had the wrong clothing and boots, one bad axe between us, and practically no rope. I was the only mountaineer in the party and when I realised how things were, I insisted that we turn back. In the end the three of us sat down, in a corrie, and argued it out. When they saw I was adamant the other two drew guns and informed me, in the friendliest way, that if I would not take them over they must shoot me. That is one way of winning an argument. We went on. I bore them no ill-will. The Gestapo had their tickets, and it was worth any risk to them to get across. At least, I hope it was, because less than twenty-four hours later the rotten rope between us parted like a piece of string at the wrong moment and they both fell four or five hundred feet on to the rocks. I reckon they slept more softly than they would have done in one of Heydrich's prisons. I reached Hungary that evening, with bad frost-bite in both hands.

I managed to get to one of my 'safe' addresses. It was a retired dentist, who lived in a pepper-pot villa in the foothills with six dogs. I stayed there for three months. My right hand got better, but my left hand worse. In the end a doctor came out and took off the middle finger. As soon as I was ready to move I started drifting south again.

Hungary was quite different from Czechoslovakia. The Germans were the big influence all right, but they weren't in military occupation. That didn't come for another eighteen months, when they walked in at the front door at almost the same moment that the Russians came in at the back; and then things really did get lively.

At the time I crawled in over the northern frontier, Hungary was an artificial oasis of phoney peace. In a lot of ways it was much trickier for me than a country under occupation. There was no Resistance movement to help me. When I left the friendly dentist I drifted down to Buda and hitched up with the floating population of spivs expatriates and little criminals. The fact that I spoke Hungarian was a help. I made money by giving language lessons. By that time I was competent to teach in English, French, German and Polish. I told a complicated story, involving an American father, a German grandfather and a Polish grandmother. It wasn't my story that kept me out of goal. It was the fact that I kept on the move. Sometimes I would find a bed in one of my new friends' flats. The real trouble was that each block of flats (back at school again!) had a 'house-master' whose duty it was to report all strangers to the police. That made it terribly dangerous to stay in any flat for more than one night. When I couldn't find a bed, I slept in the open air. If I hadn't anything else to do by day, I went into one of Buda's many Turkish baths. I found a sort of restful anonymity in nakedness.

It couldn't last. The onset of winter drove me under cover. Beds grew scarcer. In the end, because I had no alternative, I stayed for a whole week with a known criminal. That was asking for trouble. I was arrested in the first days of November.

I spent a week in the Tolonzhaz (which was the House of Detention) and was then moved over to the Margit Prison for a proper going-over. In the interval, presumably, somebody had been making enquiries about me. The trouble was that I had told too many stories. When I now reverted to the simple truth, that I was a British officer, a prisoner of war, who had escaped from a prison camp in the Reich nearly two years ago, it just got a big laugh.

Memory, which has a complicated mechanism of self-protection, has drawn a curtain over a lot of that time. I think it lasted fifteen weeks. My most vivid recollection does not concern me at all. It was Christmas morning. Christmas of 1942. The window of my cell opened on to an interior courtyard and by a contortion I could look out of the tiny opening. (It was forbidden, under severe penalties, but I did it occasionally, to keep my will in order.) I heard the most inexplicable noise outside and took a quick look. A party of warders was standing in the middle of the courtyard watching a circle of prisoners—they were mostly old men, and, I think, Jews—going round and round, in the snow on hands and knees. It was like some ghastly children's game, and was conducted in complete silence. When it was finished the prisoners stumbled to their feet and were whipped indoors and there was nothing left except a beaten path in the snow.

In the new year, I was moved, with a few other prisoners. No one told us where we were going, but I was quite certain, in my own mind, that we were being taken out into the country to be quietly disposed of. If I hadn't been sure of it, I should not have taken the risk I did. We weren't handcuffed, but there were more guards than prisoners. As the train was rattling along, at quite a fast pace, through the wooded country, south of Buda, I threw myself through the window. The guards made the mistake of trying to grab me instead of shooting me. By the time they had got hold of their guns again I was rolling down the embankment and they had been carried past me. I don't know how soon they managed to stop the train, but by that time I was in the comparative safety of the woods, my clothes torn to bits, but all in one piece.

I walked through those woods, by night, for three nights. My sojourn in the Margit Korut hadn't made me any fitter and on the morning of the third day, when I could only just crawl, I crawled into Lisa's garden.

Lisa's father is a professor of toxicology and a remarkable man. He hates the Germans and the Russians, but the Russians more, because he recognises them as the real danger. He fears no one and behaves according to his lights.

I stayed there for six months, nominally hidden at the back of the loft (which was where my bed was put) but actually living as a member of the family. I stayed six months because it took me that time to get fit. I had picked up some bug in prison which attacked my stomach. Professor Prinz injected me with different by-products of kaolin, and insisted on my taking plenty of exercise. "If you lie about," he said, "it encourages the germs." So I chopped wood in the back yard. It was touch and go, but in the end this novel therapy won out, and I got back my weight and strength.

In early September I left them and walked through the country south of Pecs and down to the Drava, which is near the Jugoslav Frontier. I swam the river one warm night with my clothes in a bundle on my head, and dressed on the other bank. It was my third war time frontier crossing, and, as it turned out, much the easiest.

The Professor, who thought on international lines, already knew a good deal about the rising star of Tito and his introductions steered me into the great man's entourage. Here the first person I spoke to was an officer in my own regiment, who had been seconded to the Partisans. I had never really liked him before (I shall suppress his name) and I liked him even less when he assumed, without consulting me, that my one desire would be to help him fight his part of the war.

"But my dear fellow," he said, "you're an English officer. Fate has sent you here."

"I'm sorry," I said. "But I'm not playing. All I want now is to get back to England and sleep in my own bed." (I think the truth is that I was suffering from a cumulative morale breakdown, more insidious than any physical upset and taking a lot longer to get over. I should not assert with any confidence that I've entirely got over it to this day.)

In the end, and with very bad grace, I was taken to the coast and put back across the Adriatic in a returning M.T.B. Naturally nobody hurried themselves over me and it was mid-December before the wheels began to turn. I landed at Bari on Christmas Day 1943. Here I ran into someone with some sense, who put me straight on to an aeroplane and sent me back to England.

Chapter VIII

A JOURNEY IN THE PRESENT

SOME of this I told Trüe as we sat in the summer-house. The easy bits. When I reached England I had suffered so much at the hands of interrogators, official and unofficial, that I had got little sequences off by heart and they tripped out readily, like a favourite after-dinner story, worn a bit thin with repetition but nice and smooth.

When I reached the end I realised that I had two listeners. Besides Trüe there was Lisa who had perched herself on the bank behind the summer-house.

"If you're quite finished entertaining the *jeune fille*," she said, "I've got a message for you. Lady wants you."

"If it's all that urgent, you could have given it to me without sitting there eavesdropping."

"But I *love* hearing you tell it," she said. "Never, never, do I get tired of it."

"There is no need to sneer," said Trüe. "And he was telling it to me, privately. Not to you."

"I am sorry if I intruded. Next time I must knock."

I left them at it. In the hall I met Major Piper. He was coming down the stairs and looked pleased with himself.

"Morning, Waters," he said.

"If you've been talking to Lady, as I gather you have," I said, "you are perfectly well aware that my name is not Waters."

"Matter of fact," said the Major, "knew it all along. See you soon."

He tripped away down the steps into the forecourt, whiffling his stick.

Buffoon.

By the time I reached Lady I was in a cold temper.

"Before you start telling me what I can do and what I

can't do," I said belligerently, "let me tell you something. I've made up my mind. I'm going to see Thugutt tonight. All I want from you is a decent map and I can find my own way."

"Of course," said Lady. "But why a map? I had already arranged for a guide."

"Oh, you had, had you," I said, feeling deflated, and looking for some further cause of offence. "About time too," was all I could think of.

Lady grinned like a cat. It always pleased him to get someone on the wrong foot.

"The delay is regretted. Normally this journey affords no difficulty at all. There are men in the frontier trade who make it six times a week. But recently there have been complications. Unforeseen complications."

He wandered across to the map.

"Unofficially the frontier has been shut. Unofficially, but quite effectively Why, I do not know. The Hungarians have staged an exercise for their so-called Western Army. It has been going on for three days."

"Just why should that worry me? I don't want to go into Hungary at all. Thugutt lives in Jugoslavia."

"That would be a valid argument *if* the frontier was a nice straight line and *if* it were on the plain. Unfortunately it is far from straight and far from flat. In fact the only easy way to Thugutt's used to involve *two* crossings of the Hungarian frontier. That is now impossible. But we are not idle. An alternative route has been worked out. It involves its own hazards. I think you will find it amusing. I believe that rock climbing is one of your numerous accomplishments."

"When do I start?"

"Young Franz Schneidermeister is taking you. He will be here at seven o'clock."

I thought a bit about footwear and decided in the end to stick to my rubbers. It didn't look like rain, and anyway I couldn't have got hold of a set of nails and broken them in by seven o'clock that evening. Franz turned up to time and we set out. He was a pleasant youth, and had, as I soon noticed,

all the tricks of the mountaineer's trade, including the deceptive, short paced, shuffling stride which seems slovenly on
the flat but takes you up mountains at a pace you need to be
very fit indeed to keep up with.

He didn't talk a lot. We started by making a long cast back,
into the foothills, striking almost due West, and keeping off
all roads. Then, very slowly, we veered south, and began to
climb. We must have made a seven mile point from Obersteinbruck (it was every bit of ten on the ground) before we
halted. We had reached an outcrop of rock, shaped like a fish
standing on its head; and here we rested, and Franz smoked a
cigarette.

"Harder now," he said, with a grin.

We turned almost back on our tracks and began to climb
steeply. Night had come whilst we rested. The moon would
not be up for another two hours. I kept one eye carefully on
Franz's white shirt collar, which bobbed before me in the
darkness like a rabbit's scut and the other on my footholds.
It was difficult to judge, but we seemed to be running head
on into a wall of rock.

Suddenly, incredulously, I found I was treading on railway sleepers.

It wasn't old, disused line either. The metal rail of the
single track was gleaming in the starlight.

Franz stopped for me to catch up with him and we squatted
down beside each other.

"Where the hell does this line go?" I said. "And what
construction gang of angels flew up here with it? Don't tell
me it takes us through the mountains into Jugoslavia."

Franz was enjoying my bewilderment.

"It goes through the mountains—yes. But not into Jugoslavia. No. We are in Jugoslavia already."

"Come again."

"We crossed the frontier line ten minutes ago. It is not
always along the peaks. Here it lies on this side."

I knew enough about European-style frontiers to realise
that this might be true. Not all frontiers in Europe—in fact
very few of them—are marked with fence lines. Usually

they are invisible to the eye of anyone except the carto-grapher and the diplomat; and in mountain country the actual custom and control stations lie well back, in the foot-hills.

"Where do we go from here, then?" I said. "And what's the snag?"

"The snag," said Franz, "is that." He indicated the cliff face which stretched across our front. It must have been the result of a geological fault. It looked sheer and dangerous.

"If we go round it, we run into trouble. Guards at both ends. So we go through it."

"By the railway tunnel?"

"Yes."

"Sounds all right," I said. "Lead on."

"It is far from all right," said Franz, seriously. "And you must listen very carefully to me and do what I say. First, you must understand, it is not a passenger line. It is a working line for the Gold-Kranz High Ore Mine. Second, if they did not need this ore very badly, I do not think the tunnel would be used at all. It is more than a mile long, and has no ventilation except at the ends. There is a pump which drives the air along, but that does not always work. Last year a train broke down. The driver and his assistant were both dead when they reached them."

I swallowed twice and said, "All right. We'll just have to hope the ventilation doesn't break down tonight."

"That is not the greatest danger," said Franz. "One of the reasons we made such a long detour was so that I could watch for trains. It is a single track. There is only one engine used. If we had seen a train go past, in either direction, we should have been safe for six hours."

"I didn't notice any train," I said, thoughtfully.

"No," said Franz. "No train. We just take a chance, yes?"

"Do they run at night?"

"Sometimes at night, sometimes by day. There is no time-table."

"What do we do if a train comes? Run ahead of it?"

"If a train comes, you must throw yourself forward, quite

flat, against the side of the wall. You will be in the angle, you understand. There is no room to lie beside the track. And throw your arms above your head. That way you will occupy less space."

I looked hard at Franz to see if he was joking. He seemed quite serious. When we reached the tunnel I began to believe him. The people who had cut it had not wasted an inch. The engines were diesel-electric, and there was no smoke disposal problem, and therefore very little head room. There was very little room anywhere. The tunnel had simply been tailored to fit the engine.

"We walk on the right," said Franz. After that we stopped talking, and started walking.

Whether the air-drive was working or not I don't know, but before I had gone a hundred paces I was pouring with sweat. It was easy going, if somewhat lopsided. My left foot was on the sleepers. My right in the very narrow channel between the end of the sleepers and the wall.

The darkness was more than absolute. It seemed to take on a positive quality of its own. If you shut out every scrap of light from a room, and then shut your eyes, and then put a black cloth over your head you would get a notion of it. When I looked down at my watch the figures were startlingly bright. We had been walking for ten minutes. It was at that moment that I knew that a train was coming.

At first I had thought it was my imagination. I had been hearing trains inside my head ever since I got into the tunnel. Then I found that I could see Franz. A faint glow of light was diffusing the absolute darkness. Then the rail began to shake beside my foot.

When Franz looked back over his shoulder it was light enough to make out the expression on his face, and I saw, with a sick start, that he was afraid. I realised suddenly that all his glib talk about the tunnel was second-hand. He had never been this way before; or else he had never been caught in it.

"Could we not run?" he said.

"Useless," I said, sharply. "It's travelling five times as

fast as we are. We'll do just what you said. And get down *now*. We don't want to be spotted."

I thought, privately, that being seen was the least of the dangers. The engine carried a single headlamp, slung rather high, and even if the driver had been looking down, the edge of the track must have been in bewildering shadow.

I was flat on my face, half of me pressed against the wall and half against the granite chips of the rail bed. I wished that I had had a few minutes to scratch out even the shallowest of graves.

Noise, and more noise. Light and the smell of hot metal.

Alphabet forward. Alphabet backwards. Kings and Queens of England.

Things I have said all my life, when waiting to be hurt.

I reached William and Mary before the engine got there.

The only thing I was not prepared for was the built up pressure wave, which hit me, and, I thought for a wild moment, actually lifted me, clear of the ground.

A hot iron finger passed up my back.

Then a roaring diminuendo; and comparative silence.

Shakily, we climbed to our feet. Ten minutes later we were in the open. My coat was hanging loose from my shoulders. Some projection from the engine had caught it and ripped it from hem to collar. I rolled it into a ball and hid it in the bushes.

"Now we climb," said Franz.

It was a difficult little piece of work and it put us both back into humour with ourselves. We were climbing sideways out of the mouth of the tunnel—presumably to avoid a guard post in the opening of the valley. I could have done it alone by day. By night, I am not sure. The moon was a help but it would have taken time to make out the holds, and any sort of difficult climb is best done with a quick, smooth rhythm.

Following Franz was a pleasure. Once or twice, to start with, he looked back at me, but as soon as he saw that I

could handle myself he went straight ahead. There was a
piece of chimney work near the top that wouldn't have been
out of place on the Tiger's route on Clogwyn d'ur Arddu.
Then I could feel the summit ahead of me, and the soft
breeze of dawn.

We rested for ten minutes. Without my coat it was too
cold to stop longer. Then we started slowly down. First the
bare rock, changing to undergrowth, and after that the dwarf
pines of a nursery plantation. When we came out of the woods
the dawn was on us. The sky lightened and a streak of red
ran across the eastern horizon; then, with almost tropical
speed, the sun was up, chasing the long, black shadows to the
west.

Franz said, with a grin: "Ready for breakfast, Major?"

I noticed that we had come to the top of a man-made
pasture. Lower down, peeping from a fold in the ground, was
a chimney.

It was a log cabin, solidly but prettily built with its carved
and painted shutters, standing on a shelf, one end cut back
into the lee of the rock. A pocket handkerchief of flower
garden spilled down from the open side.

I was so enchanted by the picture it made that I did not
at once realise that Franz was worried.

"What is it?" I said.

"Why no smoke?"

"Perhaps they are not up. It's very early."

"There should be smoke," said Franz.

We slithered down the stony path, and went up to the
door. Franz knocked. There was complete silence.

He turned a very white face.

"There's something wrong," he said. "He has a dog. A
wolf hound. He at least would have heard us."

"Perhaps they are away." I was whispering too.

Franz pushed on the door. It swung open. The main room
was quite empty, the fire cold. For forms sake we climbed
into the attic, and then came down and looked into the
lean-to. Then we came out again, and looked at each
other.

"I hope," said Franz. "I hope—" He stopped, and added quickly. "There was a little girl, you see."

I had known, for some minutes. Now I was coldly certain.

(It was evening, and I was back, in a forest in South Poland, peering from the undergrowth at a ravaged farm.)

The beast had placed his foot down on that upland clearing. I could almost smell the fresh spilt blood.

It took us an hour to find them. They were in a shallow grave, under the turf at the bottom of the garden, the child and the dog with them. They cannot have been more than twelve hours dead. They looked very peaceful.

We put the turf back and let them lie. It was a pleasant place, and they were together.

In the early afternoon we started back.

This time we took no chances. We lay up in the bushes overlooking the tunnel mouth until the train had gone through. Then we followed after it. I knew it must be all right but even so I was sweating before we started. There was no point in making a big detour on the way back, so as soon as we got out we went straight down the hillside. Just under the escarpment I spotted a small white stone, which may have been a frontier mark.

It was scrambling more than climbing and an hour of it brought us out of the woods, to a vantage point.

Far below us, artificially small, Steinbruck huddled against the river. On our upland shoulder the sun still warmed us but the shadows had already reached out to envelop the town.

A violent spasm of shivering took hold of my whole body. I could keep no part of me still and the sweat was running in a cold stream off my face.

Franz said: "It is nothing. A night's sleep will cure it. If you do not fancy the castle, I can lend you a bed."

"Lead me to it," I said, between chattering teeth.

We turned off the path a mile or so, I judged, above the castle. A few yards inside the wood stood a cottage which might have come straight out of Hans Andersen. An old lady opened the door to us and cackled at the sight of Franz.

H

He said something to her in dialect and I found myself sitting in front of a fire with a bowl of hot milk.

Ten minutes later I was in bed, and dropping down. Down a'down the deeps of thought. I seemed to turn, three times, right over in the air as I fell; into a pit of unconsciousness that was deeper than any sleep.

Chapter IX

GHEORGE OSSUDSKY

WHEN I woke up the next morning and went downstairs, the cottage was empty. I waited round a bit, but nothing happened except that a black cat walked into the room, sneered at me, and walked out again. Probably my hostess of the night before.

I left the cottage, and found my way back to the path and, after one or two false casts, struck the main path down to the castle.

When I got there it, too, was practically deserted. I went up to my room and shaved and changed my shirt. I took two looks at my own bed, but Franz was quite right. One good night had done the trick. As a matter of fact, apart from a pricking behind the eyes I felt rather fit.

I made for the Operations Room. The anteroom was empty but I heard a voice speaking from the sanctuary, and went in. It was Gheorge, sitting at Lady's desk and looking a bit like the office boy who has been left in charge whilst all the bosses were on holiday. He grinned quickly when he saw me, and then went on talking.

Someone at the other end of the line seemed to be worried. It was one of those booming telephones and I heard a good round German voice saying that something "must be stopped. If it wasn't stopped at once there would be trouble." Gheorge said "Certainly, certainly. Herr Lady was down right now talking to the Chief of Police."

Then he rang off.

"What's the trouble?" I said.

"There's always trouble," said Gheorge. He looked almighty serious behind those horn-rimmed glasses, and very young. "It's the Werkebund."

"Come again."

"They were Nazis. Now they call themselves the Workers' Friends. They do nothing but make trouble."

"Workers' Friends are like that all the world over," I assured him. "What particular trouble?"

"Last night they had a meeting in the Sportzplatz. There was a fight. Windows got broken."

"Doesn't sound a great deal to get excited about."

"No. But when it was over there was a dead man."

"Dead how?"

"He did not die of excitement. His head had been knocked in."

"And you think the row was staged to cover his killing?"

"We are sure of it. He was one of Schneidermeister's men. The second to go in a week."

"Let's be plain about this," I said. "Schneidermeister and his boys are smugglers. Right?"

"Yes—that is right."

"And when you want to pass a messenger over the frontier—into Jugoslavia or Hungary—you use their services. They act as sort of couriers."

"Yes."

"The other side probably know that, and don't like it much. So they hit back—through the Nazis."

"You make it sound splendidly simple," said Gheorge, with a tired smile.

"If there is more to it," I said angrily, "why not tell me about it? If you insist on treating everyone round here like ten-year-old boy scouts, you'll only get the sort of help ten-year-old boy scouts would be likely to give you."

The telephone saved Gheorge the embarrassment of answering. This time it was Lady.

Gheorge told him that I was back. I thought Lady sounded a little surprised, but it may have been the telephone. He asked to speak to me.

"I'm glad you are back," he said. "Will you please tell Gheorge everything that happened. Good or bad."

"Most of it was bad," I said. Lady ignored this.

"Tell it to him slowly," he said, "and see that he makes

notes. When you have finished, come down to Steinbruck. I am at the Gasthof Hirsch. I have a job for you. Are you willing?"

"I'm a little worn," I said. "As long as it isn't too energetic, I expect I'll make out."

"Very well," said Lady. "In one hour, then."

Then Gheorge got out his notebook, and I talked to him. He had some shorthand system of his own. We didn't waste much time over the journey. He seemed to think our adventures in the tunnel funny. "When I went that way I had no trouble," he said. "Perhaps I am thinner than you."

One thing struck me as odd—not perhaps at the time, but when I was thinking it over afterwards. The scene at the cabin did not seem to shock Gheorge at all. I had thought myself hardened, but to me there was something inexplicably horrible about it. The little family, stamped out, buried, obliterated. All because a message had reached them which they might have passed on. Gheorge seemed to find nothing in it. Nothing extraordinary, nothing nauseating, nothing pathetic. And once again I looked curiously at him and wondered just what lay behind his youngish white face and his thick-rimmed glasses.

He was interested in detail. How had they been buried? Did I know how they had been killed?

"There was no struggle," I said. "My guess would be that two or three men came to the cabin the evening before, enough to kill the dog and man and woman without trouble, then I suppose they went up and killed the little girl. In her sleep, perhaps."

"Yes, that would be the way it would be done, I expect," said Gheorge.

When I couldn't take any more of this interrogation I said good-bye to Gheorge. As soon as I was gone, he would start to type it all out neatly, in triplicate. One for the files of the Equipe Lady, copy to Washington, copy to London.

I found Lady in the foyer of the Hirsch. He was talking to a tall, grey man with a face like a tall grey horse.

"That was the mayor," said Lady, and I thought this was so funny that I started to laugh; and when I had started I found it hard to stop.

"It's all right," I said at last. "Very difficult to explain. An English pun. Let's skip it."

"I'm glad you preserve your sense of humour," said Lady, sourly. "Now, if you are able to attend to me, perhaps I could explain."

"All right," I said. "Explain away. Anything I can do, count on me. Philip the Reliable."

"You know we have been having trouble here."

"Gheorge told me something about it."

"Good. Do you know a man called Wachs?"

"I've seen him."

"Has he seen you?"

I reflected. "I don't think so. I've no reason to think so; no."

"Could you make friends with him?"

"Make friends with him," I said, doubtfully. "I don't think he's a very friendly character."

"If you exerted your charm?"

"Quite frankly," I said, "I should think he'd be as easy to charm as a warthog with piles. If it will help the cause I'll try. But there is one person who already knows him quite well. Mitzi. I don't know her real name. Major Piper's secretary."

"Yes," said Lady. "I fear she would not be of much assistance to us. She is not reliable."

"You mean she has been seduced by the enemy."

"I do not think it was a question of seduction. She has worked for them from the beginning. That was why they procured her a job in Major Piper's office. And instructed her to make herself available to him."

"Does he know?"

"Of course."

I felt that I was being stupid.

"If he knows, why hasn't he got rid of her?"

"Why should he. They would only attempt to place another

one. That one he might not know about. He would be worse
off then. Surely that is obvious."

It sounded about as obvious as Alice Through the Looking
Glass. I said: "I'll see what I can do. I can't promise anything.
It's just possible I might be able to get a line on Wachs
through the friend of a friend."

"Splendid," said Lady, and added, insincerely. "Don't get
into trouble."

As you won't need telling, as soon as I left him I made for
the Marienkirche. Messelen had a big wooden bowl of bird
seed in his hand and was feeding his birds. We talked about
nothing in particular until he had finished.

Then I told him what I wanted.

"I know Herr Wachs," he said, "and like him not at all.
Why do you wish to know him better? And why do you wish
me to help you?"

I had, of course, seen that this one would come and had
given a certain amount of thought to it. I had decided on a
limited amount of plain speaking.

"I've been sent out here," I said, "by our Government, to
keep an eye on things. There has been trouble in this town—"

"Steinbruck was constructed by nature for trouble,"
agreed Messelen.

"Naturally, I don't want this talked about. But equally I
can't ask help unless I tell you what I am doing."

"You are Secret Service?"

"I am accredited to the British Foreign Office for Intelligence work."

"That means Secret Service?"

"If you insist."

Messelen said, "I do not think I shall help you."

I must have looked a bit blank, because he added, "There
are two reasons. First, I do not like trouble, I had plenty of
trouble in the war. I want no more. Second, I am a business
man. What you propose does not go well with business. I
may wish to sell Herr Wachs a tractor. What then?"

"I don't think he is an agriculturalist," I said. "Never
mind. Will you forget what I said?"

"I will forget it. And I will give you a piece of advice. Go to the Post Office."

I could only assume that this was some sort of code. I looked blank but receptive.

"In most Austrian towns the centre of the black market is outside the Post Office. There are men who seem to have no business but to hang about there all day and talk to people and make telephone calls. Herr Wachs is usually there. His associates also."

"I'll try it," I said.

I'd been past the Post Office half a dozen times before without noticing anything in particular, but when I used my eyes I could see at once what Messelen meant.

Like most Austrian Post Offices it had a fairly large outer foyer with four telephone kiosks and a couple of benches. Outside the doors were other benches. There were half a dozen men hanging round, two of them writing things in notebooks, two arguing, one picking his nose and one doing nothing. As I watched them, Wachs came out of one of the telephone booths, said something to one of the arguers (a tall, thin, man in a Panama hat) and dived indoors again. The note-takers closed up and a general argument took place. Wachs reappeared and said something else, and three of them went in.

Just like the Stock Exchange.

I found myself a seat in an Espresso across the way and watched. People came and went, but there were three regulars. Wachs was one. Panama hat was another. A third was a dapper little type with a dark chin and a face like Joey the Clown. The way he carried on I wouldn't have been surprised if he'd done a couple of back springs or stood on his hands. He acted as runner to the group, and kept darting off down side streets and reappearing. Once he came back with a lady's handbag, and pulled out the compact and pretended to powder his nose. This kept them in fits for five minutes.

I was so engrossed with watching them that I only gradually became aware, without looking round, that someone had sat down at my table.

When I turned my head, it was Messelen.

"Come to see the fun?"

"I've changed my mind," said Messelen. He looked, I thought, a little sheepish. "If you try this alone you are bound to make a mess of it. What is your plan?"

"Flexibility," I said. "I mean, I haven't got one. How long does this go on?"

"They'll have finished business for the day soon."

"We might follow one each, and see where they go."

"They've got eyes in their bottoms," said Messelen. "I was afraid you'd do something like that. That's why I came along. And it is unnecessary. I have been making some enquiries on your behalf. I have ascertained where they go in the evening. It is a small cinema, called the Blue Cinema, near the outskirts of the town. I have been there only once, to my knowledge. But I recollect that it is on the ground floor of a big building with an office block above it. Also I think there is some sort of club in the rooms behind it. A photographic club, something of that sort."

"Not bad, for one visit."

"I remember it," said Messelen, seriously, "because it occurred to me at the time that it was one of the least attractive places I have ever set eyes on."

"It sounds terrific," I said. "What is your plan?"

"Not my plan. Yours. I bring you information. You make the plan."

I thought hard for a moment. The trouble was that I was quite uncertain how much of what Lady had told me was confidential and how much was common knowledge. I compromised.

"What we think," I said, "is that Wachs & Co. are not only racketeers. They've got a political slant as well."

"You mean that they are Nazis?"

"Neo-Nazis was the term I heard used."

"They smell the same by any name. And there is no secret about it. Any form of gangsterism would suit them. National Socialism was founded by gangsters for gangsters."

There was such unusual bitterness in his voice that

I wondered whether some personal motivation was at work.

"It isn't only gangsterism," I said. "The idea is that the Russians may be using them. You know that there is a regular border traffic from here, into Hungary and Jugoslavia. There are probably a lot of people involved, but one of the big crowds—a crowd which was, incidentally, very helpful to us—has lost two good men in a week."

"So," said Messelen. He sat staring at me. I would have given a lot to know what was going on behind his wooden face. "I heard something. The last death, I thought, came of the riots."

"The suggestion is that the riot was stage-managed to cover the killing."

"It would be a well-worn technique. Now, what comes of all this?"

"My ideas are still flexible. But it did occur to me that someone of the group—Wachs, if he is the head of it—must some time report to his contact. If we could find out who that contact is, it would be a step in the right direction."

"It would be a big step. But—I do not wish to exaggerate —almost impossible. These men have a thousand contacts. Their business is contacts. You saw them at work this morning. There are many different ways they could meet an agent, to receive orders, or pass on information. They could write to him, telephone him, meet him in the street, at the cinema—"

He paused for a moment and our eyes met.

"I wonder," I said. "There must be some reason for choosing a cinema as their meeting place. It's mad, of course. But it would work. You go in separately when the place is half empty, sit at the back of the circle, talk to your hearts content."

Another thought struck me.

"Suppose the messenger is a girl. You can sit in the quietest corner with one arm round her. You could glare at anyone who came near you."

The table was shaking. It was Messelen laughing. "I knew

as soon as I spoke to you," he said, "that you were a romantic. Shall we proceed to the cinema tonight? I the swain, you the girl—"

I started to get angry, and then I laughed too.

"I'm damned if I'm going to dress up as a girl—although, in fact, I did once go to a hunt ball as a blonde for a bet and had the most peculiar suggestions made to me by a drunken Colonel—but if you're game for a visit to the cinema, I'll come."

Messelen sat, for quite a long time, silent and looking out of the window. In the light of early evening his normally pleasant face had a grim, set look. Wachs and Co. had disappeared and the square was almost empty.

"It's quite mad," he said at last. "It will do no good, and may land us in trouble."

It was himself he was trying to convince, not me. I leaned on the other side of the scale.

"They don't know you," I said. "And I've no particular reason to think that they know me. I'm new on the scene and I've never interfered with them."

"I think you have not yet quite realised. This is not England, where every man sits secure in his own back garden, with policemen in the streets. Here you are close to the end of the world. The place where the water gathers speed and goes over the black cliff."

"What you want is a drink," I said.

"All right," said Messelen. "I'm behaving like a maiden aunt. I'll come with you, but one thing I insist on. You must change your clothes. It is not a high class place."

"What do you suggest?"

"Something old, but not too shabby. You are not to dress up as a workman in a play, you understand. I suggest you should seem to be respectable but poor."

"A blue suit with shiny elbows and knees, a thin black tie and a cap."

"That should be admirable. Can you find such clothes?"

"Yes; I think so."

"Then we will meet at my flat. Tomorrow? Very well. At

eight o'clock it will be beginning to be dark. And one other thing. Have you a gun?"

"I'm afraid not. I might be able to borrow that too, but I'm no sort of shot."

Messelen looked surprised. His ideas of the British Secret Service had evidently received a blow. "I will see if I can find you a gun," he said.

Chapter X

HERR WACHS AND OTHERS

In the end I decided it would be better if I took Gheorge into my confidence. I asked him to get me the outfit.

He jotted it all down. Gheorge was the perfect Personal Assistant. If I'd said I wanted a bottle of arsenic and a time-bomb he'd have got them for me. Or a thumb-screw; he'd have written that down too. He might have asked "Left or right hand thread?" He was a chap who liked to get things right.

When we came to footgear he suggested "Workmen's boots?" But I said no. I'd wear my ordinary light rubber soled shoes. They mightn't be in character, but I hate anything heavy on my feet.

"Light shoes are a disadvantage in a fight," said Gheorge. He might have spent half his life kicking people in the stomach.

"I don't aim to get into a fight," I said. "I'm not the fighting type. What I'm best at is running away. Nice light shoes are best for that."

"All right," said Gheorge. "When do you want it?"

"By tomorrow evening. We're aiming to get to the cinema some time after eight."

"I'll have the stuff in your bedroom by six o'clock."

"I'd be obliged if you could handle it yourself. The less people who know about this the better, I should think."

"You don't mind if I tell Lady?"

"Not even him," I said, firmly.

Gheorge looked as if he was going to object, then broke into one of his rare smiles. "I can see," he said, "that you are beginning to have a proper appreciation of our work."

It was a few minutes before eight on the following evening

when I knocked at Messelen's door. He was standing beside the table cleaning the grease off a small automatic pistol.

"It's a Mauser Kindchen," he said. He showed me how the clip went into the handle, and I loaded it once or twice to get the hang of it. "I should judge that it's most effective range is two paces."

"That sounds just my style," I said. I put it in my pocket, where it swung a little, but felt comforting.

Messelen was wearing an old black suit. He looked as solid and as reliable as the Rock of Gibraltar.

"He's my plan for this evening," he said. "Unless you have anything better to offer? No? Then we'll go in my car which we park near at hand but, I rather think, not *too* near. There is an alleyway about a hundred yards short of the cinema—I went down this afternoon to have a look. From there we will walk along and join the audience. If we see Wachs, or anyone else that we recognise, we will try to keep in sight of where they are sitting and follow them if they leave."

"And at the end of the performance?"

"I had it in mind that it would be better if we came out just before the end. One to watch and one to bring the car up. We should then be in a position to follow whatever happens."

"That sounds all right to me," I said. And added: "What I really mean is that it sounds absolutely mad, but I agree that it's the best we can do. We certainly don't want to get behind Wachs and breathe down the back of his neck."

"I have discovered something about the other two men you saw. The little one who behaves like a clown is an Italian from Carinthia and his name is Tino. No one knows much about him except that he does no work and has a lot of money and spends it all on girls."

"The Welfare State in a nutshell," I said. "What about the tall one?"

"He is a less pleasant character. His real name I could not discover. He is known as the Margrave. And his specialty is the knife."

"Wachs, Tino and the Margrave," I said, thoughtfully.

"I can really imagine nobody I would rather spend a quiet evening without. Let's get going quickly or I shall come to my senses and return home to bed."

Messelen did not smile. He arranged the covers over the brass cages, closed the big window carefully down, so that it was shut all but a few inches, and wedged it with a wooden wedge. Then he took a last, thoughtful, look around to see that all was in order, and turned out the light.

His car, a handy little black Opel, was garaged at the end of the close. As we backed out and turned into the main road the great bell of the Marienkirche was announcing the half-hour.

The main streets were brightly lighted, but almost empty. When we turned off towards the eastern quarter the street lighting ceased. At first there were one or two lighted shop fronts. Then even those fell behind, and we had to use our own lights discreetly.

"Here is the place," said Messelen. He had called it an alley; it was really an open courtyard between two tall buildings. We ran into it, switched off, and locked the car.

"Down this street, right at the end and then—hullo. What's this?"

Messelen, who was walking ahead, stopped so suddenly that I bumped into him.

"What is it?"

"Police cars."

We had reached the first corner, and looked round it. In the next street three cars and a tender were packed nose to tail. There was a driver in the first one. The others seemed to be empty.

We crossed the road, and strolled down the farther pavement. The driver looked blankly ahead of him, but I knew he had seen us.

"Don't like it," said Messelen. "What are they up to?"

Before we got to the second corner, Messelen said "Down here. Don't hurry." He seemed to have a surprising knowledge of the by-ways of Steinbruck. The alley we had got into twisted and turned until I had lost all sense of direction; then we were looking out into a better-class street.

The Blue Cinema lay some twenty yards up and on the opposite side of the road. Across the road, between us and the lighted foyer, was a barrier of trestles. There were half a dozen policemen there, and they were stopping everyone who went by. Farther up the street, beyond the cinema, was a second barrier.

Across the side street which ran down behind the cinema was a police car, and there were policemen at the front and side entrances.

As we watched, a man and woman came out. They seemed surprised at the reception committee. A few questions, and they were passed along to the barrier. Someone wrote something down, the barrier opened, and they went through.

"It must be quite a film," I said.

Messelen said nothing. I could tell that he was worried. Presently he touched me on the arm and we crept back the way we had come.

When we were safely in the car I said (the relief in my voice was probably only too evident): "Well that's the end of that. Since the local force has chosen tonight for a Cleaner Films Drive there doesn't seem to be a lot we can do."

Messelen said: "I can believe in a good many things, but in a coincidence as big as that, no."

"What do you mean?"

"Tell me. Who exactly have you taken into your confidence about our trip tonight?"

"One person only."

"And he is?"

"A character called Gheorge. He's Lady's personal assistant. I had to tell him roughly what I was up to to get hold of this outfit."

"I see." Messelen's breath came out slowly.

"Just what are you getting at?" I said, patiently. "Do you suppose that immediately my back was turned Gheorge rang up the local police and asked them to parade three deep round the cinema just to prevent us getting in? Why should he? And even if he had asked them, why should they have done it?"

"I just don't believe in coincidences," said Messelen. I had never heard his voice so ugly.

"Whether you believe in them or not," I started to say, felt his hand on my arm, and stopped short. Then I heard them too. Measured footsteps coming towards us, from the direction of the Cinema. They came nearer, hesitated at the corner, and then swung towards us.

"Duck," said Messelen. There wasn't much room in the car, but we got our heads down as far as we could.

The steps came slowly up to us, went past. I could hear three men. The smell of cigar smoke drifted into the car.

"So you don't believe in coincidences," I said into Messelen's ear, which was a few inches from my mouth.

"Get out quietly. See if you can spot their car. I'll be turning. Catch you up."

By the time I was out, the three men were gone. I ran to the corner and looked up the street. They were moving, quite slowly, away from me; Wachs I would have known anywhere, and the tall knife expert; the third man was a stranger.

Messelen had turned his car, and its bonnet came to rest by my left elbow.

"I'll follow on foot," I said. "When I've gone a reasonable distance, bring the car up to me."

"Das Bockspringen. Good."

"If they turn a corner I'll wait for you. The only trouble is, they may hear the car starting and stopping behind them."

"They're talking pretty hard. I think it's the only way."

I scudded after them. That part wasn't difficult. There were three of them in boots, going slowly. I was in rubber soles and alone. Once when the road forked I thought I had lost them but Wachs' blessed cigar suddenly shone out like a beacon.

"Cloud by day and fire by night," I quoted blasphemously to myself.

The trouble was I could hear Messelen's car every time it started and stopped. I was nearer, of course, and was listening for it, but I wondered it didn't penetrate their talk. Once

I

I thought it had. They all stopped and seemed to look back and listen. At that moment we had a stroke of luck. Three army lorries rolled past. By the time they had got by, Messelen was up with me, his engine safely switched off.

"I've got a feeling they're wise to us," I said.

"Don't think so," said Messelen.

"Then why have they stopped?"

"My guess would be their car's near here. I was right. Jump in. Now we're off."

A pencil of light crept out of a side-turn and swung away from us. It was a big old-fashioned machine. So much I could see in the silhouette of its own lights.

As soon as the three men were aboard, it swung away, gathering speed as it went. How we hung on I know not. We were the disreputable little terrier that has got its teeth into the tail of the greyhound.

We never, of course, used our own lights. I had time to notice that we were going east, out of town, and towards the frontier; and that we seemed to be passing through an interminable area of vineyard. Then we were clear and climbing. The white road unrolled, the red light ahead of us swayed and darted like an uncertain shooting star.

Then it blinked, slowed and disappeared.

Messelen trod on his brake, and we pulled up in a swirl of our own dust.

"It's a private house," I croaked. "Driveway. Some sort of lodge gates."

"Must get clear of the road," said Messelen. "See if you can find an opening."

I scrambled out and ran back. A short way down the road I found a field gate. It was wired, but I lifted the wire off and pushed it open. Inside there was a rutty track which looked as if it would take a small car.

Messelen was already backing. A neat turn, and he brought her in. I shut the gate behind him and got back into the car.

"Run fifty yards and stop," I said.

The track swung in, towards the house, and I thought for a moment it was going to bring us back into the grounds.

Then I saw that there was a thick belt of wood ahead of us.

We stopped under a tree, and as soon as the engine was switched off the silence and the darkness dropped back over us like a warm cloak.

I said, "It looks as if we may have pulled a fifty-to-one chance out of the hat. We can't be more than a couple of miles from the frontier. A lonely house like this in its own wood—"

"It is possible," said Messelen.

"You don't sound terribly happy about it."

"I dislike the obvious. Let's find out where we are. There's a map in the door pocket in your side."

I found the map and handed it to Messelen. He unfolded it on to his knee and turned on the dashboard light, which gave a single flicker and went out.

(On such small things hang our lives.)

"Bulb," said Messelen. "Curse." He fumbled in his pocket pulled out a cigarette lighter and clicked it on. It wasn't much use for reading maps by. The yellow flame jumped, flickered. Then I remembered.

"I've got a torch," I said, breathlessly. "Gheorge insisted I take one. Sensible chap, Gheorge. Hold on a moment."

The light from my torch cut across Messelen's hand, on to the map.

"Where did you get that lighter?"

"Curious, is it not," said Messelen. "But pleasant. A girl gave it to me. Hold the light steady."

My hand was shaking. I snapped off the light.

"What is it?"

"It sounded," I said, with a conscious effort, "like footsteps. Might have been imagination." But I knew it was not imagination. I was out on my own now, and everything was real.

Very gently I eased open the door on my side of the car. Then I bent across to Messelen and whispered, scarcely moving my lips, "Watch that patch of darkness ahead." He nodded, and I stepped out on to the grass.

The blood was drumming such a devil's tattoo in my head that I could hear nothing outside.

I moved round, came back again on Messelen's side, slipped my hands through the open window of the car and got him round the neck.

Messelen was a much bigger and heavier man than me, and stronger in almost every way, but his body was wedged into the bucket seat, and that took away nine tenths of his advantage. He couldn't even bring his knees up.

A rock climber is not a gymnast, but his life may hang on his wrists and his fingers. Mine were the strongest part of me, and training had doubled their strength.

Even then, if Messelen had been able to think, he could have saved himself. His best chance would have been to have sounded the horn. That would have brought his friends running. But it is difficult, even for a brave clearheaded man to think, when life is going out of him.

He made the mistake of trying to pull my hands off. He might as well have tried to unlock a bolt without a spanner. Then, but too late, he went for my face and eyes. I buried my head in the small of his back. He could only catch a piece of my hair, and that he pulled right out. I think I laughed at that.

At the end of two minutes, his body had stopped threshing, and in four I was sure that he was dead.

I shifted the body across to the other seat, and got in beside it. Then I started the car, turned it and started back towards the gate. My hands were shaking so badly that I needed both of them on the gear lever to change gear.

At the gate I stopped. I realised the danger, but there was nothing I could do about it. It took an age to get the gate open, and another age to get the car out onto the road. Messelen had swung in with one confident movement. It took me four shots, backing and starting again each time to get out on to the road and pointed back towards Steinbruck. I must have left a track like the entrance to a tank lager.

As I got going down the road, I thought I heard a car starting, either in the woods, or in the grounds beyond. I had no attention to spare for it. Something was wrong with my wrists and if I got up any speed at all this was translated into a horrid wheel wobble.

Luckily the road was straight, down hill, and absolutely deserted.

"Get off the road," said the monitor inside me. "Stop behaving like a fool and get off the road." I was running back in to the vineyard area which I had noticed on our way out. There was a gate on the right. I swung round towards it. It was a single gate and it may have had some flimsy sort of lock. I butted the radiator straight into it; the gate gave way, and I was headed down a flint gravel path.

Ten yards along I stopped, got out, walked back, and lifted the gate back onto its catch. It didn't seem to be much the worse for its experience.

At that moment I heard a big car coming. Heard, not saw; because it was carrying no lights. I went down flat on my face and stayed there until it was past.

Then I got up, walked back to Messelen's car, and drove on. I hoped that the path led somewhere. It wandered down, between the rows of the vines, which sprawled in a patchwork along the side of the hill. Presently I had gone far enough to be out of sight of the upper road. Below me, a long way below, I could see the silver line of the river. I drew up and saved myself the trouble of switching off by clumsily stalling the engine.

I have no idea how long I sat, in the blessed silence and starlight. I could hear a passing and repassing of cars on the upper road and once I saw the fan beam of what looked like a searchlight. But no one came near me.

I was in baulk.

When my thoughts began to run consecutively I found I was thinking about my first meeting with Messelen. How I had come into the room and had seen him, standing, with the sun behind him, in a blaze of quiet glory. And how I had liked him. That was the bitter thing. Just how stupid can you be?

It was absolutely plain to me now; the steps by which he

had led me on; his well judged reluctance to help; his tit-
bits of information, each one served up at the exact moment;
his "no, you make the plan. You're the leader. I'll play
second fiddle" (In fact, he the conjurer, me the stooge).

What had been his plan for me that night? First, I judged,
a very unpleasant reception had been awaiting me in the
Blue Cinema. It could have been almost anything. The cards
were stacked for them. It was their stamping ground.

Gheorge, good patient Gheorge, had put a stop to that.
It had been a word from him which had had the cinema
surrounded, and had caused my enemies to remake their
plans on the spur of the moment. A miracle of improvisation.
All the same, if I had not been asleep, besotted by my
confidence in Messelen, I must have seen the raw edges and
the joints. (However hard three people were talking, could
they walk through those silent streets and fail to hear a car
starting and restarting behind them? People like Wachs and
the Margrave. People who only remained alive as long as they
remained suspicious?)

But I had swallowed it all. When the fish is once on the
hook he does not easily fall off.

What had been planned for the final act? A stealthy ap-
proach to the house. A quick coshing. A quiet disposal of the
body. Good Lord, they need not have troubled themselves
about that. I could have been left to lie. What was I, a
foreigner, unaccredited, in disguise, with a gun in my pocket,
doing on private property at that time of night? Lady might
have guessed the truth. He could have done nothing. He
would have done nothing.

And how pleased Captain Forestier would have been.
How pleased everyone would have been.

A little shiver ran through me, and I found myself smiling.
If I was starting to feel sorry for myself I was, indeed, cured.
For I well knew that I had no reason for complaint. On the
contrary, fate, in that last moment, had dealt me a fifth ace,
right off the bottom of the pack.

If Messelen had not taken out his cigarette lighter I should
now have been as dead and as cold as he was.

I leant over him, felt in his side pocket, and pulled it out. It was a heavy, chased silver lighter designed in the shape of a book.

I knew it well. I had given it to Colin Studd-Thompson on his twenty first birthday.

I climbed stiffly out of the car and looked about me. I knew, now, roughly what I wanted. It took me ten minutes search before I located the vigneron's hut, away to my left, down a side track. The door was on the latch, and inside were mattocks and spades. I was careful to touch nothing, and I had my handkerchief round my fingers before I would even lift the latch.

I made my way back to the car. I had noticed a pair of chamois leather drivers gloves in the dashboard locker and I got them out and put them on. If I had been stupid so far, I must try to redeem it by extra care from now on.

There was a rug on the back seat. I folded it across my back. Then I got Messelen out, and up onto my shoulder. He was heavy, but my mountaineer's technique helped, and I was confident that I could carry him down as far as the hut.

When I got there I laid him carefully, on the edge of the flint path.

The moon was well up now, and by its light, I looked around for the exact spot I needed. The careful vigneron fights a year long battle, hoeing and digging and clearing the soil round the roots of his beloved vines. I wanted a place where the soil had been turned recently, but not too recently. I found the exact spot, some fifty yards down the hill and set to work.

First I spread the car rug on the path. Then, using a spade, very very carefully, I took off the top layer of earth and piled it on the rug. Then I got busy with the mattock and hollowed out a shallow grave. It had to be shallow. The ground was too hard for deep digging. I got down about two feet.

Then I laid Messelen in his grave. Before doing it I searched his pockets but got nothing more for my pains than an automatic pistol, a doorkey and a handkerchief.

Then I piled back the undersoil, pressing it as flat as I could; then I added as much of the dry top soil as would go in without leaving a hump. I slashed lightly across the whole area with the mattock. Not just the grave but a good piece around it as well. There was a bit of top soil left over. I dragged if off down the hill in the rug and sprinkled it broadcast among the vine roots.

When I came back past the spot where I had been digging I had genuine difficulty in locating it. Only morning would show if I had made a good job, but I fancied that if no one came with too critical an eye for twenty four hours, Messelen might sleep there undisturbed till doomsday.

When I had polished the spade and mattock and put them away and got back to the car the stars were pale and the light of morning was coming back. Also a mist was creeping up from the river.

I still had a lot to do.

First I took off the brake and started the car downhill with a push. I guided it for about twenty yards along the path. Then I went back and examined the place where it had stood.

The flinty, chalky, soil which had been such a hindrance to digging was here a godsend. There were light marks of the tyres in the dust, but nothing permanent; nothing that a single farm cart or even a stiff breeze would not wipe out. I took a particular look to see if the car had dropped oil or left any other sign of where it had stood, but I could find nothing. There were one or two footsteps, where I had got out, but I brushed these over with the folded rug.

I then set to work on the car itself. First I went over the bodywork, holding the left hand glove in my gloved right hand and using it as a polisher. Then I shook every bit of earth off the rug and folded it back onto the seat.

The next thing was to find a way out. Forward, if possible. The car would leave marks if I turned it, and I didn't really, fancy my chances on the upper road.

I had one or two bad minutes as the path wound and twisted its leisurely way down the slope. Once I thought it was petering out altogether; then I saw the turning, and shortly after that a gate. It led me out to a farm track. The gate was not locked.

Dawn was coming upon me in great strides. I ran the car slowly along the track until I could see the farm. The track went slap through the middle of the farmyard. It was quite a big place; probably the farm which owned the vineyard.

At the very last possible moment, I cut out the engine. The gradient was steep enough to carry me through. A dog barked twice, angrily, and then, with my last remaining momentum, I had swung round the corner and was out onto the main road.

I looked at my watch. It was five past four, and here came the mist, both to help and to hinder.

I had reached that stage of fatigue when my eyes were playing tricks, and twice I braked as shadowy vehicles loomed down on me, only to fade into nothingness as I stared at them.

I got to the Marienkirche, through the ghostly streets, as the bells sounded out the half-hour. I had seen no one; nor, I think, had anyone seen me.

I parked the car as nearly as I could remember the way that Messelen had parked it, switched off, and sat for a moment to think.

There were one or two things at the back of my mind. Things that I ought to do before I went home. My mind wasn't turning over very fast, and the bell sounding the three quarter hour brought me up with a jerk. First, it warned me that if I didn't keep moving I should sleep; and at the same time it started a useful train of thought.

Messelen was a solitary man. It might be some time before he was missed. Therefore, and plainly, the more doubt about his movements the better.

I climbed out of the car, eased the door shut, and stole into the house. Messelen's front door opened to the key I had taken from his pocket. I left the door on the latch, and put the key on the mantleshelf. Then I went round the bird cages, carefully lifting off the cloth squares which covered them. The birds were very quiet, and the big, yellow, cock-bird looked at me out of one eye as if he knew what I had done.

I got out the bowl of seed and piled up their dishes to overflowing and filled up their little water troughs. I reckoned they had enough to get by on for a day or two, probably longer.

Then I took out the gun Messelen had loaned me. I was pretty sure what I should find, but I examined it to make certain. The clip was all right, and the bullets in it looked genuine. I took it right out, pulled back the firing slide to eject the round in the breech, and then pulled the trigger. Nothing happened at all. I looked at it again. The spring was there, but the pin had been removed.

I polished it off carefully in my gloved hands, reloaded it, and put it back in the drawer of the table.

Then, after a final look round, I tip-toed back the way I had come, and was soon clear of the town, headed into the blessed mist.

I have no recollection of reaching the castle, but Lisa says that she was up early and saw me from her window. She says she knew from my walk that something was badly wrong and that she ran down and opened the side door for me; that I walked straight past her without a word, with a face like death, and went up to my room.

Chapter XI

FERENC LADY AND THE FACTS OF LIFE

I BOBBED about for a few uneasy hours on the surface of sleep and waking. I dreamed no dreams; I was not deep enough for dreams. I knew that the hours were going by, and the shadows lengthening on the wall and I heard the small sounds as evening came on and the castle woke.

It was a barking of dogs which finally pulled me back to reality. I slipped off the bed, feeling for a moment that sort of spurious lightheadedness that comes when I am really tired, and walked across to the window.

Three storeys below, Tutti and Lippi came bounding out of the postern gate and caracolled off into the woods with Trüe behind them. She was taking them for their evening outing.

I ran a basinful of cold water, pushed my face into it, and held it there until I was seeing red spots, and then pulled it out and gave it a towelling. Then I combed and brushed my hair, hard. It made me feel a little better, but not much.

When I got down Lady was waiting in the anteroom. Waiting for me, I guessed.

"How did you get along with the Major last night?" he asked.

"All right."

"A rough party?"

God damn the man. What was he hinting at? Quite suddenly I realised that he wasn't hinting. He knew. My first reaction was anger, followed, in a photo finish, by alarm, and then relief.

Lady stood watching me, perched on the fender, grinning all over his face like a pert young crow.

"Better come inside," he said "and tell poppa all about it."

"I suppose it's no good suggesting you mind your own damned business?"

"No good at all."

"Who told you? Gheorge?"

"Of course Gheorge told me. It would be a funny sort of organisation here if he had not done so."

"In spite of the fact that I only told *him* under pledge of secrecy."

"You're talking like a boy scout," said Lady. "Have a cigarette. Oh, no. You don't do you? Then just relax and reflect, how lucky it was that Gheorge *did* keep me informed."

"It was your people who put a police cordon round the cinema?"

"Our powers are not quite as extensive as you seem to imagine, but a word in the ear of the Austrian police sometimes produces results."

"Just what was due to happen in the cinema?"

"It's a little difficult to predict, but I rather think that you were going to make an indecent assault on a young lady and her escort was going to hit you, and there was going to be a small, but high-class fight. Messelen would have got away with a black eye and possibly a sprained wrist. But you—alas —I fear, you would not have survived."

"The Rœhm technique," I said. "If you plan to murder a man, be sure you take away his character first."

"Oh, certainly. The Major was a Nazi to the boot-heels. But do not underrate him. He was a high-class operator. His real name, by the way, was Felder. You remember?"

"Faintly," I said.

"He was one of the luckier ones at Nuremberg. Not quite enough evidence for a capital sentence. He was not one of the biggest shots, you understand, but well up in the third rank."

Memory stirred.

"He was the Hauptmann Felder who carried out the Pinzio massacre."

"Alleged," said Lady. "Alleged. He carried it out so

thoroughly that absolutely no one was left to testify against him. With their characteristic respect for the laws of evidence, combined, no doubt, with admiration for a workmanlike job, your compatriots voted for his acquittal. The Russians would have hanged him. He received two years detention on lesser charges, after which he worked unceasingly against the British, who had saved him, and for the Russians, who would have hanged him. Not an uncommon reaction."

"A neo-Nazi?"

"Of course. A founder member of the Werkebund."

"He fooled me," I said, "to the top of my bent."

"His appearance was an asset," agreed Lady. "The simple soldier. And indeed, I believe, in his early years he was precisely that. A simple, brave regimental officer. So was Goering."

I wasn't listening. I was thinking of the first time I had met him, in that clean room, full of sunshine, with the cathedral bells chiming and all the birds singing.

"What was the programme that first evening?"

"Oh, the standard technique. If you had gone inside Major Piper's office, I do not think you would have walked out again. Messelen's story would have been that you had got drunk, which was true."

"Partly true."

"And had tried to interfere between some man and girl, and the man had assaulted you. Possibly thrown you downstairs. A broken neck. What easier?"

"How very fortunate," I said, "that Major Piper should have arrived when he did."

"Oh, very," said Lady. "Very."

"And now, perhaps, you will explain two things that I find puzzling."

"Of course."

"Why, after all that, did you allow me to go out with Messelen last night, in complete ignorance of his real character?"

"That is only one question."

"The second is even more curious. When you spoke,

just now, of Messelen. You said: "He *was* a high class operator" and later, "His appearance *was* an asset." You spoke of him in the past. Almost as if he were dead. I find that curious."

Lady looked at me for a long moment, and I thought, for the first time in our brief acquaintance, that I could detect a hint of uncertainty in his manner.

Then he smiled, a big, simple, frank smile; frank as any expert witness under cross-examination.

"Why," he said. "Don't tell me I was mistaken after all. Did you not kill him?"

"Yes, I killed him,"

"You had me worried for a moment," said Lady, relaxing. "But if that's right, what's the mystery?"

"The mystery," I said, patiently, "is how you knew anything about it. You knew I was going out with Messelen, because Gheorge broke his word to me and told you. You knew about the cinema, because that's something you arranged. But nobody on God's earth can know what happened afterwards."

"It would perhaps be exaggerating to say that I know."

"Don't fool yourself. You couldn't even guess. It was one chance in a thousand that anything happened at all except my death."

"I wouldn't put it quite as high as that. After all, consider the chances. The Major was not a heavy smoker. But he was bound to take out his lighter sooner or later."

I said stupidly: "He didn't use it to light a cigarette. It was to look at a map. *How the hell did you know?*"

"Of course I arranged for him to have it."

"You *what?*"

"Try not to be obtuse. I arranged for him to have the lighter. I had it given to a girl, with instructions to give it to him—not earlier than yesterday morning. The danger was that you might see it too soon."

I could feel my anger getting hold of me. Only it was the wrong sort of anger. The cold and comfortless anger that roots in fear.

"Would you mind telling me what the devil you mean."

"I shall tell you nothing if you make a scene about it."

"You'll get no scene from me," I said stiffly. "Just tell me the story. Where did you find the lighter?"

"It was picked up, on Pleasure Island, by one of my men, on the night Studd-Thompson disappeared. We knew it was his. Trüe had seen it many times—"

"And you had it planted on Messelen so that I should see it and lose my head and kill him. Before he could have me killed."

"Your synopsis is accurate, with one exception. I did not for a moment imagine that you would lose your head. Or, if you lost it I knew that you would recover it very quickly. Perhaps you would be agreeable now to telling me what happened last night."

"Why should I?"

"Why should you not?"

"Because—" Fury came bubbling up in a great cold wave, like the seventh wave of seven, taking away my breath, overwhelming me, blinding me—"because for all I know, as soon as it served your purpose you will inform the police about me, as easily and as quickly and as treacherously as you have broken every promise you have made since I came here—"

"And did I ask you to come?"

That pricked the bubble. I subsided into a chair, feeling limp, and with nothing left to say.

"You must also remember—" having achieved his effect Lady performed another of his lightning changes and became sweet reason itself—"that you who are, you will pardon the expression, an amateur, have elected to play a part in a match of professionals. A match which is played to its own rules, of which you know nothing at all."

"And want to know nothing," I mumbled.

"Nevertheless I will explain the rules to you. I think you have earned it. The first is that you trust no one unless you are forced to. The second is that you tell no one anything unless it pays you to do so. Pays *you*, not him. When an opponent at bridge gives up a trick, you do not say: "How kind of him." You ask yourself: "Why did he do it? What future advantage does he hope to gain?" The third—"

"Spare me the third."

"The third is even more important. You start from the assumption that anyone might betray you. Anyone. Not only your opponents but your associates as well. In any organisation such as this it pays to base every plan on the absolute assumption that your opponents will have succeeded in introducing one of their side in to your team, or more simply, in corrupting one of your team."

"Like Major Piper's blonde secretary."

"Oh, yes. Of course, Major Piper knows she is a spy. And by now, she knows that he knows. Her employers would replace her, if they could, but Major Piper will not dismiss her because he knows where he is with her."

"Also," I suggested, "because she is his mistress."

Lady considered this. "I can see no logical connection," he said.

"I have always been lead to suppose that the female spy seduced the Intelligence Officer so that he would babble his secrets to her when in her arms."

"Your ideas are old fashioned. Now when I am in bed with a woman I never speak at all. I—"

"All right," I said. "We'll leave it there. I take it, from what you say, that you have a traitor here."

"Of course."

"And you know who it is?"

"Well, I have a very shrewd suspicion. After all, the field is not wide. It might be our host and hostess. Unlikely, perhaps? I agree. It might be their son, the Herr General. Or the dutiful Gheorge. Or the experienced Lisa. Or the so sweet and so disingenuous Trüe." His tongue flickered for a moment between his teeth. "Or it might have been Studd-Thompson. Or it might be you."

"If a joke, a poor one."

"Or it might be me?"

"I hope you're not serious."

"Of course I'm serious. Put yourself in the shoes of our

opponents. If they wish to buy themselves an ally in our organisation, what more natural and effective than to choose the head of it."

"Really," I said, weakly. "If you had been a traitor, you'd hardly have taken the risk of suggesting the idea to me."

"I fear that your bridge playing has led me to over-estimate your mental ability. However, to business. I have a proposition to make to you. Much of what I have said has been leading up to it."

"Almost everything you have said has been calculated to make me distrust you."

"Exactly. That is why I put my proposition in the form of a bargain."

"I have nothing to sell."

"That was perhaps true, yesterday. Now it is not true. It is absolutely essential to me to know what did happen last night, after you left the cinema. You are unlikely to tell me of your own free will and I have no way of making you talk, or no quick and easy way. Therefore I will buy the information."

"For what?"

"In exchange I will tell you exactly what is going on here."

"I have been told two different stories already. How am I to know that the third will be the truth?"

"Even you should, I think, be able to recognise the truth when you hear it."

"It has a certain rarity value round here," I agreed. "Very well."

I was aware that I was placing my neck at his disposal, but there was a certain relief in getting the story told.

Lady made me describe the house, the grounds and the wood. And then identified them to his own satisfaction on one of the large-scale maps on the wall.

He did not seem interested in the precise location of the body. "A vineyard," he said. "I think that was a fortunate inspiration. The vignerons are very regular in their habits. And they have no reason to dig deep. Tell me again about the car."

K

I went over that part of it again.

"You parked the car outside his flat? Just as he had left it? And you are certain you left no prints? On the gear lever? On the brake?"

I thought hard. "No, I polished both of them. And I drove wearing gloves. That must have rubbed off any marks that were left."

"Yes. A certain amount will depend on how soon someone drives a cart down that track. What about the lighter?"

I took it out of my pocket and handed it over.

"The incinerator, I fear," said Lady. "Am I now to fulfil my part of the bargain?"

"If you please."

"For myself, I should be delighted. It was you that I was thinking of. What I have to tell you really *is* a secret. It is at present known, in full, to perhaps six people in Hungary, and a dozen in the West."

"I should feel privileged to join the circle."

"Yes," said Lady. "Do you carry poison?"

My feelings must have been apparent because Lady smiled. "It is quite a simple precaution," he said. "No real trouble, and not as dramatic as it sounds. Studd-Thompson, I know, did so. In a very small, metal, container which could be braced without discomfort to the inside of his mouth. He took it out at night, I understand."

"Just like dentures," I said. "Suppose you tell me the secret and let me judge what precautions are necessary for its preservation."

"Very well," Lady sighed. "You will understand me when I say that military espionage is now almost as out of date as the bow and arrow. The last people to recognise this are, of course, the military intelligence departments. But it is nevertheless a fact. The days when Mata Hari lavished her charms upon senior generals and extracted from them, between the sheets, the tonnage and performance of the latest tank are, alas, gone. Nowadays if we want a military secret we buy it. It is a question only of paying sufficient. Either in money, or in kind. And even if this were not so, you will agree that it is futile to expend blood and effort in obtaining information which will be out of date six months after you have obtained it."

"So what do you do?"

Lady said: "It has been called psychological warfare and it has been called propaganda. In Communist circles it is sometimes referred to as mass indoctrination. I have a simpler and easier word for it. I call it interference."

"Right," I said. "They interfere with you. You interfere with them. More particularly you interfere with Hungary. You throw Spanners into Works."

"Exactly."

"And what particular spanners are you now engaged in throwing?"

"It is, of course, axiomatic that you attack an opponent where he is weakest. The weak spot of the regime in Hungary, as you may know, is the industrial worker. He has a scarcity value. There is not enough of him to go round. It gives him a bargaining position."

"Well that's the way it works in the weak-kneed Western democracies," I agreed, "but I fancied that totalitarian countries enjoyed certain powers of persuasion."

"You can take your horses to the water. They will not always drink. Do you know that last winter, so short were they of miners, the Budapest police were driven to round up criminals, gypsies—prostitutes even. It was not a success."

"I should have thought the miners would have loved it."

"After a number of unfortunate incidents the women, any-way had to be released. But you can judge from that—which, by the way, is absolutely true, I have a most reliable in-formant in the coal mining centre at Pec—how vulnerable the government is likely to prove on its industrial front."

I thought about it. It seemed to tie in with what the Baron had told me.

"Just what are you planning?"

"A General Strike."

The words floated quietly out. From Lady to me. Into my head and out again. Through the windows, over the trees, across the mountains, across the plains.

The words turned into ideas and the ideas into pictures. Half a dozen men in a small back room, smoking and talking. A knot of workmen meeting in the shadowy corner of a huge workshop. A crowd in an open place, in the rain, listening to a man in a rain coat, talking, talking, talking. The rain drumming on the cobble stones. The crowd surging and breaking. The drumming of the rain changed to the metallic chatter of machine guns.

A man screaming.

"How can you keep such a thing secret?"

"You cannot, altogether," agreed Lady. "The Hungarian Government know of the danger of industrial unrest. They must be aware that agitators are increasingly active. They may even suspect that they are being subsidised and encouraged from abroad. But exactly what we plan and when and how—that much I think is still hidden from them."

"Do they know of *your* connection with it?"

"There are signs of uneasiness. The troop movements I mentioned look like an attempt to seal this particular section of the frontier. And yet, I don't know. We shall see."

"When and where does it start?"

"That is a thing that David Szormeny would give up to the half of his treasury to know. I think you would be happier without the information."

On reflection I agreed.

I can't remember if anything more was said. I had a lot to think about, and I think better if I move, so I walked in the garden, in the twilight. The bats were out, swooping and fluttering. I find them no more sinister than mice or cockroaches. My cousin Michael's old rectory is full of all three.

My mind was on strikes. I had never considered them before from the view point of the strike-maker. The fomenting of strikes was traditionally one of the things that the Communists did to us. Not we to them. And yet why not? If that was the new warfare, must we not learn how to wage it?

Not trumpet and drum, but the manifesto. For powder and steel, the ballot box and the vote. For poison gas, the human voice. Arise, Hungarian proletariat. Cast off the chains of your bureaucratic masters.

After dinner I made myself unpopular again by refusing to take a hand at bridge. I walked out and sat on the terrace. What I needed to do was think.

Mostly I thought about Lady. It gave me an odd and unpleasant feeling to think that he should have used me so calculatingly. Something of surprise, something of annoyance, but a distinct touch of fear, too, no getting away from it.

That he should have sent me out, so cold-bloodedly, hoping that I would kill Messelen for him, but not caring if, in the process, I lived or died! Granted he had no reasons to love me, for I had butted, unasked, into the delicate mechanism he was controlling. But that he should have commuted this into a positive feeling of dislike was the uncomfortable thing. Had he disliked Colin in the same way? It was quite possible. Despite his frankness that afternoon he had not really explained what Colin's part in the enterprise was meant to be. Had Colin outstayed his welcome too, and been expended by his host in some equally cold and forlorn experiment?

I got up and looked through the window. Lady was sitting with his back to me. As I watched he selected, with great care, the two of clubs from the remaining cards in his hand and laid it on the table.

Lisa, who had taken my place, looked unhappily at it, dithered for a bit, and played the ace.

I dragged my feet upstairs to my room. I was confident that I should get no sleep.

When I opened my door I stopped. There was a patch of lightness on my bed where none should have been.

"Don't turn on the light," said Trüe.

When I got further into the room and my eyes grew accustomed to the darkness, I saw that she was sitting up, in the middle of my bed, wearing my pyjamas.

"Who told you you could wear those?"

"No one."

"Take them off at once."

"But of course."

I was wrong. I slept very soundly that night.
And for some nights to come.

Chapter XII

TRÜE

I AM certain that outwardly my relations with Trüe did not appear to change at all. But Lisa, of course, knew.

Only once, in the course of that week, did she say anything about it. I was alone on the terrace and she came and sat down beside me.

"You find Trüe sympathetic," she said.

"Very."

"Be warned then. She had Pisces in her horoscope."

"And that, I suppose, makes her a slippery customer."

"You must not laugh at the planets."

"I don't laugh at them," I said. "I just don't believe in them."

"How can you not believe them, when what they say comes true?"

"If you go on making predictions long enough, a few of them are bound to come true, in the end. By the law of averages—"

That started a wrangle, as had been my intention.

(My relationship with women had always followed that pattern. I start by loving them, truly and wholeheartedly, until, in time, they come to love me. Then I get frightened. Or tired? The cynic, Claude Anet, said "*Aimer, c'est difficile. Être aimé, c'est fatigant*". Only a Frenchman could have said it, but there might be a particle of truth in it).

So far as Trüe was concerned I never had time to get beyond the blissful first stage. Possibly she was destined the big exception in my life.

When I think back over my time at Schloss Obersteinbruck I find that I can remember the early days down to the death of Major Messelen in detail, day by day. After that my impressions begin to blur. If I take pencil and paper and a calendar I can sort it out, but I can't remember it.

It must have been about halfway through that week that Major Piper drove up behind me as I walked through the Square and invited me to jump in his car.

"What's this?" I said, as I got in beside him. "Arrest?"

"A year ago I might have said 'yes' to that," said the Major. "Now I'm just a military attaché. No executive powers. A sort of diplomat." He gave a little, snorting laugh, at the thought of himself as a diplomat.

We drove down to the river. The Raab, which joins the Feistritz ten miles lower down, has here been artificially broadened out to a shallow lake. The stream is unnavigable above the town by anything bigger than a canoe, but below the town small motor launches run down to the junction on the Hungarian border. Little sailing boats, their white sails gleaming in the sun, swooped across the water on both sides of Pleasure Island. At this time of the morning the bandstand was empty and the side shows were shuttered, but the strip of beach was alive with sun-brown children.

"Pretty, isn't it?" he said.

"Smashing. What did you bring me here to talk about?"

Two very bright, but very worried eyes looked out at me from under the sandy tufts of the Major's eyebrows. When I had first met him I had thought him a fool. I realised that I I had been wrong.

"The Austrian police have been getting at me," he said. "They seem to think that you've killed somebody."

"Did they say who?"

"Yes. A man who called himself Messelen. Real name Felder."

"Had they any reason for their suspicions?"

"You had been going about with him a good deal lately. And were seen with him in his car the night he disappeared."

"Isn't it rather shaky reasoning? He had plenty of other friends."

"Policemen don't work by reasoning. They go by information received. Someone has given them a straight tip. They say you knocked Felder off and buried him. They've been doing a bit of digging."

"Where?"

"Oh—all over the place. In the woods and fields."

"They've got quite a lot of ground to cover."

The Major looked at me and said: "You're a cold blooded fish, if you'll excuse my non-diplomatic language. By the way, did you know you were being followed?"

"No. Who by?"

"The police. They tagged onto you as you came into the town. Out at the castle you're in baulk. Lady's outfit has got a sort of diplomatic immunity. But they'll pick you up as soon as you step out. There he is. Twenty yards back, on the other side of the road."

There was a grey car there, all right, with a middle aged driver, cutting his nails. He didn't look like a policeman.

"Not a bad thing really," added the Major. "From your point of view, I mean."

"If you say so."

"The lesser of two evils. If the police weren't there, I expect Messelen's friends would try to get at you. Dirty crowd."

We sat for a moment, watching the children on the beach. Two small boys were trying to drown a smaller one. Like children all the world over.

"I'll do what I can for you, of course," said the Major, at last. "You'll excuse me asking, but is this sort of thing quite your cup of tea?"

"Intelligence work?" I said. "From what I've seen of it, it makes muckraking respectable and sewage-disposal clean."

"It's not all it's cracked up to be. Like war but without any of the chivalry or trappings. Necessary in its way, I suppose. It did occur to me to wonder—not that it's my business—but is there any reason why you shouldn't cut adrift and go home?"

"Not really. I came to find a friend of mine. But I'm beginning to believe he's dead. I'd go tomorrow, only Lady seems to want me to stay."

"I see," said the Major. He started the car and turned it towards the town. "It's your life."

The driver of the grey car put away his nail scissors and came round behind us in a leisurely curve.

It wasn't that afternoon but, I think, the following one that I happened to interrupt Lady at work. I had gone in to talk to Gheorge and I found the three of them there. Lady in his shirtsleeves, heels up on the table, cigarette holder in mouth, listening, and Gheorge and Lisa with pencils and note books out.

As I came in they waved me to silence. There was a crackle of atmospherics, and the wireless receiving set in the corner said, in Hungarian: "David Szormeny speaks".

Lady nodded. Gheorge reached out and pressed a button and I heard a soft whirr of the monitoring tape recorder.

Then a voice.

My Hungarian is exact, if not colloquial. I listened held, in spite of myself, by the unseen speaker. (I have always thought that there is an art of oratory which is quite independent of the spoken word. The art of the hesitant beginning, and the calculated pause; the variations of tempo, not so slow as to numb not so fast as to bemuse; the introduction of each new theme; the careful crescendo; the stupendous finale. It seems trite to compare a great speech with a work of music. It *is* a work of music. A solo for the finest and most variable instrument ever created, the human voice.)

Szormeny used facts as rivets, not as ballast. They had a clenching force, but were driven in sparingly and, once in, were somewhat difficult to locate.

Subversive forces, said his voice, had been at work, encouraged and, in some cases, directed, by agencies outside Hungary. The head of a certain neighbouring state (he would name no names) had seen fit to make public utterances casting aspersions on the heads of the Hungarian government. That was a sort of mud-slinging match in which he, Szormeny, would not join. For himself, he had no fears. He would submit himself to the only tribunal that mattered. The people of Hungary. All that, however, was the past. Now that the harvest was successfully brought in, it was an appropriate moment to face the future. The latest statistics of trade and industry were highly encouraging—

I looked at Lady who made a guttersnipe gesture.

—There had been a certain amount of quite artificial unrest, in the heavy engineering and transport sections, but it had now been proved beyond a doubt that this was inspired by a pitiful organisation of emigré malcontents working from outside the border. Let them but set foot in Hungary, and the people's democracy would demonstrate in unmistakable fashion what they thought of such activities—

I tried to visualise the man behind the screen of his words. It was not easy. The words themselves poured out, heavy, smooth, and controlled. But was there something in the tone of voice; something intangible, but nevertheless there; the faint but mocking side tone of a voice which says less than it means.

I felt, as I listened, a prickling premonition of trouble.

—To our many well-wishers we would say, Hungary lives, Hungary prospers, Hungary marches forward. To the one or two who wish us ill, we repeat the old Hungarian proverb: "If you speak ill of a man, be sure first that you are out of reach of his arm". Our arm is not as weak and not as short as some people would appear to imagine. There are occasions on which it could cross the artificial borders of territory and reach the enemies who snap at its heels with imagined impunity—

I happened to glance round at this moment and so caught the look on Lady's face. It was a revelation. Clean gone was the customary sardonic humour. In its place, a flash of—yes —triumph. I was looking at a man, who, after arduous labour, after an infinity of planning, after a lifetime of deception, sees success within his grasp at last.

I have been in a number of unpleasant places in my life, sometimes in the actual face of death, but I cannot remember when I have felt the presence of danger so near.

But for a moment, only.

Then the old Lady was looking out at me again.

"You have the appearance," he said, "of a man who is

suffering from a stomach-ache. Perhaps you find Szormeny's oratorical style cathartic?"

"I should judge," I said, cautiously, "that he is a very practised orator, who says no more and no less than he intends."

"Even his indiscretions, you would say, are calculated."

"His indiscretions above all."

"You might be right." He turned abruptly to Lisa and Gheorge and said, "I should like to see the draft of your reports as soon as they are ready. If I fly to the Hague tomorrow, I should like to be able to take them with me."

Lisa and Gheorge nodded like good children, and I went away to find somewhere quiet. I wanted to think.

It was on the following day, that I first mentioned to Trüe the prospect of paying a visit to Pleasure Island.

We were lying, I remember, in the wood behind the castle. My head was on her stomach, and her head was on Lippi. My ear, being pressed against her midriff, I had the illusion that I could listen right down into the core of her. And, as I spoke the words, at the centre of her mystery, something stirred.

"Must we?" she said. "It's much nicer in the woods."

"Much nicer."

"Then why?"

"Just an idea I had. I was thinking about Colin—"

Ping! It was extraordinary. Almost like radar.

"You mean when he disappeared. That he was on Pleasure Island, with me."

"Yes. It's just a silly sort of idea I had of trying really to accomplish something before I go. Before I push off home with my tail between my legs."

"Do not abuse yourself. You have done all that could be done."

"Which is nothing."

"Sometimes there is nothing to be done. Why not go home now, Philip? Right home to England."

"Soon," I said. "I want to make one last effort before I do go. It's just a silly idea. But I thought that we would copy, as closely as possible, what you did on the evening Colin disappeared. Tell me about it again."

"There is almost nothing to tell. It was a gala night. As, indeed, it will be tomorrow—"

"Better still."

"There was a big crowd of people. In the beer garden, listening to the concert. And among the stalls and sideshows. They are nothing, really. Just booths where trinkets are sold."

"What were you doing?"

"Just sitting and listening. The orchestra was playing the finale from Rosenkavalier. You know it—?"

"Yes. I know it." It appeared we both knew it, so we hummed it in unison.

"That's right. Then Colin said to me, 'Wait here a minute. I'll be back'. And he got to his feet and walked off. That was all."

"In which direction?"

"Out of the beer garden. Towards the booths, I think. It was all very crowded."

"Did anything happen before he left you?"

"What sort of thing?"

"Did anyone speak to him? Did he see anyone? Or say anything?"

"Nothing. We were listening to the music."

"Was he your lover?"

Contact! No doubt about that one.

She said "Yes," and all her breath went out at once. My head went down with it, like the sponge, when the bath water runs out.

This time I had enough sense to tell Lady, in advance, what I proposed to do. He was past being surprised at anything.

"I will have you watched, discreetly," he said. "Also, I think, we will warn the frontier posts."

"Yes," I said. I suppose I had long since realised that, if he was not dead and buried, Colin must have been taken out of the country.

"I do not think, though, that you will run into that sort of trouble. But you had better keep your eyes open for Messelen's friends. Have you a gun?"

"No."

"You are very wise. A most overrated weapon. However, just for the evening, Gheorge will find you one."

"Do you think I am making a fool of myself?"

Lady opened upon me his most expansive smile and said: "Of course you are. But we have a Hungarian proverb, 'You will find the rainbow attached to the tail of the donkey'."

"That doesn't sound flattering," I said, and went off to look for Gheorge. I found him with Lisa. They were sitting together in the Operations Room, reading a copy of a report, and looking a lot too pleased with themselves.

"What goes on round here," I said, "that you're all grinning like cats? Has Szormeny had a stroke, or something?"

"Not yet," said Gheorge. "But perhaps he will, soon."

"He's in for a rough passage," agreed Lisa.

Gheorge seemed to think this terribly funny; I left them giggling together.

At eleven o'clock on the following evening the finale of Rosenkavalier was drawing to its raucous close.

"It is not really a coincidence," explained Trüe. "These orchestras have—what do you call it—a schedule. At the end of the month they come round again to the end of their repertoire."

"And evermore," I said, "go out by that same door where in they went."

"That is a quotation?"

"A misquotation."

"You are drunk."

"I am. But not with liquor. I am intoxicated with excitement. The night. The music. And you. Every time you lean forward I can see—"

Trüe sat up sharply, and said: "You realise that we are under observation."

" I had noticed the large gentleman at the gate, who followed us in. Yes."

"I thought also, that the tall man with the wall eye seemed interested."

"He has gone now. He was sitting at that table. Do you know him?"

"It is possible," I said, carefully, "that he was a character called the Margrave."

"He did not look very nice."

"His looks do him justice."

The last notes of Rosenkavalier sounded. The roll of the side drum merged into a burst of applause, and I said to Trüe, "Think carefully. What next?"

"You say to me, 'Sit still I won't be a moment' and you get to your feet, and you push your way across to that exit."

"And then?"

"Why, then you go through it."

"Sit still," I said, "I won't be a moment." Her eyes held mine for a second. I could read nothing in them. Hers was not an easy face to read. You needed your ear right up to her stomach to detect what went on inside that girl.

I pushed my way slowly and carefully through the crowd; family groups; no one I had seen before. The exit gave onto a corner of the island which was full of booths. There was a broadwalk down the middle, which was lined solidly with them. I had never seen them open before. They were not exciting. Some sold sweets and drink. Others were full of souvenir ash trays and stocknägel. Since very few tourists come to Steinbruck now I can only suppose that the inhabitants have got into the way of selling them to each other.

I marched down the landward side, conscientiously inspecting each booth. I even purchased a stud box with a dachshund head on the lid. Nothing sinister happened. So far as I could tell I was not being followed.

At the end I turned, and made my way along the outer side. These were the booths which backed on to the river. Quite the largest of them, in the middle, was a photographer's. It had, on a board in front, the usual display of snapshots. Serious Austrian fathers in Tyrolean hats. Fat Austrian mothers on rustic seats. Young couples in trompe-l'œil poses behind mermaids and lorelei. And, bang in the middle of them all Colin Studd-Thompson, looking serious but satisfied, and wearing an old Harrovian tie.

It looked so incongruous, it was so unexpected, that I think I stood there for an appreciable time, mouth open, and staring. I knew what it was. It was a mousetrap with a bit of cheese in it. Cheese was what I wanted. I pushed through the curtain at the entrance of the booth and went in. I was in a sort of porch. A notice said: "Please to be careful that you entirely the outer curtain close before the inner one you open."

I pushed through the inner one. The booth had more depth to it than I had imagined. In the half darkness at my end a small man was doing something with a camera. In the bright light at the far end a young man was sitting with a girl on a papier-maché sandcastle, against a background of the Rhine at Bonn.

"A smile if you please," said the little man. The man and girl smiled. There was a click. More lights came on, and he added, "That will be fifteen schillings. You can pay when you collect the prints. In twenty minutes. And what can I do for you, sir?"

"I am interested in a photograph you have in the window."

A blank look replaced the professional smile.

"I am afraid they are for display only sir. Not for sale."

"I did not wish to buy. But I could not help noticing a photograph of a friend of mine. I could point it out to you."

"There is no need. Perhaps if you describe it."

"It is quite different from the others. Not a snapshot at all. A portrait photograph, of an Englishman. It is in the middle—"

"I think I know the one you mean. Yes."

"How did it get there? Is it one of yours?"

He said, "I do not know. Perhaps it has been put there by mistake."

"But surely you could tell me when it was taken. The man is a friend of mine. He has disappeared—"

That, I realised, was a false step. There was no mistaking the look in his eyes now. It was fear.

"I do not know anything about it sir," he said. "I have many photographs. Some I take myself, but not necessarily all."

I said: "I believe you are lying." But he was not listening to me. I turned my head. Wachs was already through the inner curtain and the Margrave was close behind him. I had the impression that there were others in the outer lobby.

There was an opening in the curtains behind the studio stage and I went for it, fast. The little photographer made a bleating noise and grabbed at my jacket. It was a half hearted effort, and I had no difficulty in brushing him aside.

The man who was waiting for me behind the curtain had an easy job, but he put his heart into it. He was an enthusiast. The moment I got through he hit me with his fist, a tree-felling blow, on the bottom of my ribs.

I went back through the curtains like a tennis ball that has run into a smash at the net.

I think I should have fallen anyway, but the Margrave hooked my feet from under me, and the three men dropped on me. One of them was across my legs. Another held my arms, and the third—the Italian Tino, I think—picked up the photographer's dusty, black satin camera cover and swathed it carefully round my head.

Through the soft cloth cruel fingers found my nose and mouth.

In the next few seconds I knew death. The torture of stopped breath. The agony of a pumping, bursting heart. The tearing pain of lungs that screamed for air and were denied; and blackness shot through with red.

Then the cloth was removed, and I lay, my lungs working desperately.

"He's tame," said Wachs, in German. I was rolled on to my side, and my hands were fastened. I was too busy breathing to do much else.

A pair of hands came down towards me. They were holding a bright metal contraption. I flinched as it went into my

L

mouth; then I realised that it was a sort of dentist's gag. It was operated by a thumbscrew. The screw turned. My mouth opened wide.

"Don't break his jaw off," said the Margrave.

"Why not?" said Wachs. He stopped turning, and got out a dentist's hook. Then he gave my teeth a raking over. He found a loose stopping that seemed to interest him, but there was nothing underneath it, except tooth. He satisfied himself quite thoroughly about that.

"I'd pass him," he said. "Nothing hidden."

The metal contraption was removed.

"If you wouldn't mind telling me," I said.

A great, flat, palm of a hand came at me carrying a cut strip of adhesive plaster. It flapped across my mouth, pressed down on me. When it went away again my lips were sealed. Quite literally.

I waited for the next thing to happen. A tearing noise suggested that some more adhesive tape was being prepared.

"You put it straight over his eyes and they'll never get it off again without taking his eyelids with it," said Tino critically.

"Not a bad idea," said Wachs. A moment later I was blind as well.

"What about plugging up his nose, as well."

"You shouldn't do that. They paid for him—in advance—in good condition."

A foot rolled me over.

"He's in prime condition." The same foot kicked me. "Hardly a wriggle out of him, see?"

A new voice said something that I could not understand. It sounded like 'net'. It felt like a net, too. A fishing net. I could smell the tar and feel the cords bite into me as I was lapped in it.

Then I was lifted.

As at a great distance I heard a voice say: "See that the way is clear, Franz."

For a moment my mishandled body hung suspended. A

salmon in the landing net. Hooked, gaffed, winded. Near to
merciful death.

Then we started to move. I sensed that we were in the
open air. It was a very short journey. I was lowered on to
boards; boards which yielded under my weight.

The soft sounds of water a few inches from my ears. The
puttering of a motor. Everything sounded slow and distant
and unactual. As sense departed, I thought of the watchers
on the gates; of the patrols on the roads and the guards on
the frontier. They were wasting their time. They were
ignoring the lessons of geography. They should have grasped
one simple fact. That the Raab ran into the Feistritz. And
that the Feistritz ran into the Danube.

Part III

THE END GAME

" Each warrior picks himself a stake
To try if he the Great Beast's neck can break
Lord ! What vile creatures Fortitude doth make ! "
Battle of the Beasts.

Chapter XIII

THE PIGS' ORCHESTRA

I MUST, I think, have been unconscious for the greater part of the next three hours. Perhaps I was at no time quite unaware of what was happening but there is a numbness of the mind, equivalent to paralysis of the body.

Two impressions only remain of that time. First, I am certain that the boat which I was in pulled up at some sort of jetty; that the motor was switched off, and, in the silence, voices spoke. There was no alarm in them. They spoke quite softly. And a torch shone on the cocoon of netting in which I lay swathed. How I knew that, with my eyes bandaged, I should be hard put to it to say.

Then there was the moment when I realised that I had changed captors. It was when I felt fingers parting the netting over my face, and feeling down towards me.

Very gently the fingers came to rest under my jaw bone, against the side of my windpipe. I suffered a moment of blind terror. I could feel the pulse in my throat hammering. Then the fingers withdrew and I realised what they were doing. The man squatting over me had not been sure whether I was alive or dead.

After that, I think I slept.

When I woke again, I knew that dawn had come. I could still see nothing, but I could hear the birds tuning up for their morning overture. Everything was very quiet, and there was a feeling of wet white mist in the air. I had woken up just so many times, on camping holidays on the Broads. Then I heard another sound. A car of some sort was approaching Not a car, a light truck, or van.

The hands fumbled under me and I was lifted. Out of the boat on to the landing stage of planks; rolled over until I was clear of that net and all its knotted, corded, tarry confinement;

lifted again into the back of the truck. Two men climbed in with me, the tailboard was slammed into place, and we started off.

There are degrees of discomfort, as the prisoner in the dungeon knows. I should not normally have described my position as easy, but freedom from that net, combined with unrestricted, if petrol-smelling air, was luxury; and I think I slept again. So deeply this time, that I have only the dimmest recollection of the truck stopping and of being raised out of it.

What jerked me back to full consciousness was the strip of plaster being pulled off my eyes. Tino's genial prediction that my eyelids would go with it was not, in fact fulfilled, but it was a close thing.

I lay, blinking up, blinded for a moment by my own tears.

There was a further jerk, as the plaster came off my mouth and then, comparatively painlessly, off my wrists too. I was hoisted up into a sort of wicker chair. My feet remained hobbled.

As I lay there, like a sack, only moving my head, quite slowly, from side to side, I realised where I was. I had been in many such places before. It was a hiker's shelter-hut, of the sort that you find all over the mountains of Central Europe. Not a high altitude one, or it would have had double windows and a big stove. Just an ordinary, forest-walkers' shelter. Usually they were only opened when the snow came.

I heard a noise of crackling sticks and turned my head again. There were two men in the room, solid men, wearing workmen's overalls, but wearing also, and more unmistakeably, the air of heavy authority which officialdom stamps on her children.

So, for better or worse, I was now in the hands of the State.

The immediate change was undoubtedly for the better. The results of the efforts at the fire turned out to be a bowl of hot soup and a pot of thin coffee. I wolfed down the soup, with chunks of bread, and swallowed the coffee; and then went to sleep again, but properly this time.

When I woke up the sun was looking in at the western window, and a second meal was in process of being cooked.

I had time to observe, and began to notice things. The first thing that struck me was the confident, unworried bearing of my gaolers. It was evident that we were waiting for dusk before we went on our way, and to that extent secrecy was thought to be desirable. But they weren't worrying about it. Every move they made proclaimed that they were following through a well-worn routine. How many other recumbent bodies had polished the wicker chair in which I lay? For how many previous unwilling passengers on this curious underground railway had they heated soup and boiled coffee?

As my will climbed back into control of my body a less comfortable set of impressions began to assert themselves. The firmness, the consideration, the judicious sympathy. I had observed nurses in charge of a patient who is due for a dangerous operation. I had once, for my pains, to watch over the last twelve hours of a man before he went to the scaffold. I had also seen cattle going to the slaughter house.

What would happen if I tried to make a break for it ?

The plain answer was that nothing would happen. My feet were hobbled. I was lying back in a chair that protested my every move. There were two very wide awake gentlemen in the room. And the door, I suspected, was locked.

For our supper we ate half a dozen fried eggs. (One of the men must have been out foraging whilst I slept.) And drank some wine.

When we had finished eating, and everything had been meticulously cleaned, and the fire raked out, and knapsacks repacked, the bigger of the two men, whom I took to be the leader, came over and stood, for a moment, looking at me.

I was his payload. He was weighing me up.

Then he said in his clipped, colloquial Hungarian, that I could understand with an effort, "He looks a lot fresher now."

"So long as he doesn't get too fresh."

The big man produced from his pocket a pair of handcuffs, and fastened my hands behind my back with a quick precise, gesture. They were American type handcuffs which get tighter if you struggle. I didn't struggle.

Then he cut the rope hobble off my feet and said, in his best English, "Now we go."

It was, I imagine, the same vehicle that had brought me; the small, canvas backed, type of lorry that you see in hundreds on the roads in Europe. The driver was already in his seat. The two guards manhandled me up into the back and we started off.

They took it in turns to watch me. One would sit on the edge of the seat, his eyes on me. The other would relax and smoke. After ten minutes they changed roles. It was as professional as that.

When I was certain that I had no chance of escape I concentrated on trying to make out my whereabouts. The back of the tilt was up, and I could see the stars. As soon as I had placed Orion I knew where I was. We were going almost due north, with a touch of east in it.

This gave me food for thought. If, as I surmised, my entry into Hungary had been via the Raab and the Feistritz, and I was now travelling North, this should bring me back roughly to the place I had started from; but on the Hungarian side of the frontier.

At one point the road looped so that, for a moment, we were travelling almost South and I glimpsed the Plough and the Pole Star. I saw something else as well. It was the characteristic peak of the Radkersberg, the same that I had pointed out to the Baronin from her conservatory window. I was right then. The place we were making for was not very far on the Hungarian side of the Austrian border. I thought of Schloss Obersteinbruck, standing sentinel the other side of the mountains. It seemed very distant, in time and in place. As though at the reverse end of a huge telescope I saw the pigmy, gesticulating, figures of Gheorge and Lisa and the General and Trüe and Ferenc Lady. Lady, I am sure, was smiling.

The tyres hummed and the white road unrolled behind me like the used film off a spool. My head nodded down on to my shirt, rose with a start, and sank again.

It was the slowing of the vehicle that jerked me back into the present. We were turning off the road, into a gateway. There was a murmur of words, and we went on, still slowly, and climbing. Then we stopped altogether.

Both my guards were very much on the alert, now. Headquarters, I guessed.

Came the sound of a heavy door opening. We backed, made a half turn, and ran under an archway, and through it, into a courtyard. The same heavy door was shut. My guards relaxed. Their job was over. The mouse was in the trap.

One of them fumbled at my wrists, and the handcuffs came off. I climbed out awkwardly.

The size of the courtyard suggested that it was a very large house indeed. Something of the type of those monstrous German Spa-Hotels, which we copied from them and erected in the closing years of the last century, to the desecration of our countryside. A big, heavy, functional, soulless lump of brick and slate. The middle-class villa inflated to a castle.

As soon as I got inside I knew that I was in a police headquarters. From start to finish I hardly saw anyone in it wearing uniform, but when you've been in one or two you get to know them by the smell. I was signed for in a book ("accepted unexamined, without prejudice to damage discovered subsequently"), and my original guards disappeared still unsmiling and unmoved. I wondered what sort of lives they led off duty. I was invited to sit down and I sat, and waited. For a long time. One man sat at a desk, copying entries from one book into another. A second man sat by the door. He had nothing to do. A clock ticked.

Quietly in the distance a bell trilled.

The man by the door came out of his chair as smartly as if a sergeant-major had shouted at him, and seized my arm. Another man appeared from nowhere. I was hustled along a passage. There was a door at the end of the passage which said "Colonel Dru". This was opened and I was pushed inside

It was a huge room, something between a study and an office. There were two smallish desks behind each of which sat a serious looking young man. And a very large desk indeed, which was unoccupied. The owner of this desk was filling out a leather armchair beside the open fire.

Colonel Dru, I supposed.

He was the perfect pig-man. So perfect that you looked round for the make-up. But, no. On closer inspection you could see that this was something that nature had conceived, thought out, and executed without assistance. The skin pink but tough enough to turn a carving knife, the bristle of hair, the overflowing jowl, the little tusks of teeth and the tiny, deep set, twinkling, vicious eyes.

"Offer our friend a chair," said Dru, "and stay if you wish."

This increased the audience to four. I got the impression that the Colonel was a man who liked an audience when he performed.

"I must protest," I said, "against this treatment of a British subject."

"But of course." Dru swivelled round in his chair, placed his elbows on the arm, and his chin on his hands, like some parody of a benevolent judge. "Make your protest."

"I have made it."

"But is that all?"

"I have nothing more to say."

Dru closed his eyes, opened them again, and stared at each of his four assistants in turn. They tittered. I sat back in my chair and determined that, come what may, I would keep my temper.

"Really now, Mr. Cowhorn—"

I must have looked puzzled.

"I have your pronunciation?"

"Oh, you were trying to pronounce my name. Well, I suppose that's not bad for a first shot."

"I was saying, Mr. Cowhorn. Why have you put yourself into this business. It is not your business. Why do you intrude in it?"

"It would take a long time to explain."

"We have the night in front of us."

"I've been looking for a friend of mine."

"Admirable. But of course. His name?"

"His name is Studd-Thompson."

"And you came here expecting to find him."

"I didn't come here at all. I was brought."

"But that name. Do I not remember him? A moment."

The Colonel held up one finger, as if he was listening for the first cuckoo. His aides gaped. Turning on them, he shouted: "Studd-Thompson. Search. Search. In the cabinets. He may be here." They leapt to their feet, hauled open a filing cabinet each, and began thumbing through folders. "Quicker. He may escape. Some search under S. Others under T. Leave no stone unturned. But no. There is nothing." The Colonel sank back in his chair. He waved the others back to their seats. "It is no use. He has escaped us."

I said, coldly, "If you have any serious questions to ask, perhaps you would be good enough to ask them."

"But of course I am serious. I have asked you a question. Why do you interfere in this business? Our countries are not at war. We are friends."

"Great big friends."

"Exactly. All friends together. Then why do you violate out friendship?"

"I have done nothing—"

"Co-operation. That is what we ask. If we are friends, we co-operate. If we co-operate, then there is no trouble. Am I stupid?"

He shot me a sharp look from his sharp little eyes. It was almost a nudge in the ribs.

"Oh, yes," I said. "I mean, certainly not."

"Then that is what you should tell them at the Castle. How are all the dear fellows, by the way. The General, and Gheorge?"

"They were all very well when I left them."

"Fine, fine. And Lisa? And Trüe?"

"Fine," I said. "Fine."

"And Herr Lady?"

"Well, of course. I didn't see a great deal of him," I said, cautiously.

"A great man," said Dru. "But he might have been greater still. Perhaps the greatest in all Hungary."

I was surprised to detect a note of what sounded like genuine respect.

"I had no idea." I said.

"He did not tell you? But certainly. For a year or two after the war, his star was in the ascendant. There was nothing he might not have achieved. Then he made one mistake. But one was enough."

"And what was that?"

"He refused to sleep with the Minister of Transport."

The bellow of laughter which greeted this was like a sudden attack by the wind-instruments. I looked round. The orchestra had increased to six, an old man, and a thick, black haired, unfriendly character in the uniform of a major.

"She was, perhaps, past her first youth. But not un-attractive. Imagine it. Throwing away a cabinet post from mere fastidiousness. Eh, Becker?"

Major Becker agreed that he would sleep with the rear portion of a pantomime elephant if it would advance him professionally.

The Colonel plainly regarded this as an attempt to steal his audience, and quelled the laughter with a frown.

"You see," he said to me. "We are frank with you. Why not be frank with us?"

"I hardly see what I can tell you. You know so much already. I presume that someone at Schloss Obersteinbruck is your informant."

"Of course."

"Which one?"

"You do not know?"

"No," I said. "I've no idea."

"Incredible. Quite incredible." The conductor toyed with his baton for a moment whilst the orchestra watched him starry-eyed.

"No doubt from time to time Lady informed you of his plans?"

"He told me practically nothing. And much of what he did tell me was, I suspect, untrue."

"At first, no doubt. But later on he confided in you?"

"No. Why should he?"

"Even after you had removed Major Messelen for him."

A very faint twittering from the strings. I tried to keep my head.

"Who says I murdered Messelen?"

"My information is that you strangled him with your hands and then buried him."

Major Becker said something, and Dru bounced round on him.

"You do not believe he could do it? That is because you cannot judge the finer points of a man. You would like a demonstration?"

Apparently everyone wanted a demonstration.

"Come here, then, Major."

Becker got to his feet and I had a chance to examine him more closely. He was biggish and white and had a lot of black hair, some of it on the back of his hands. He smelt of flowers. I liked none of him.

"And you."

I got up.

"Now, Major, you have strong hands and wrists? Yes. Good. Now see if you can break his grip."

We held out our hands and stood there, for a moment, like embarrassed contestants who have been forced to make up their quarrel in public. Dru beamed at us.

Becker put on the pressure. He was strong but not exceptionally so. If you hold your hand in the right way an opponent can do you no harm by hard gripping. He wastes his strength. At the end of a minute I felt his pressure weakening and sharply increased mine. Becker winced. I tightened again. He gave a little grunt, and we broke away.

Dru glanced round the room and collected the applause. I had no attention to spare for them. I was trying to remember something. Just how many people had I told that I had strangled Messelen. Lady, of course. And possibly one other, certainly no more. It looked as if the field was thinning out as we got nearer to the post.

"And now that we have all had our fun, perhaps you will answer a few very simple questions."

"You still haven't explained," I said, desperately, "by what right—"

"Have you any rights? Has a murderer any rights? Is he not outside the law?"

It was a nice point. But I suddenly felt tired of it all.

"What do you want?"

"Information."

"According to you I have no information. You know everything already. Far more than I do."

"Not everything. And in any event corroboration is always useful."

"And what makes you think I shall tell you anything?"

There was a pause of pained surprise.

"But *of course* you will tell me," said Colonel Dru. "When I ask for information I obtain it. Do I ever fail?" He glanced round. There now seemed to be nine people in the room. "No, Colonel," they said. "You never fail."

"Are not my successes well-known?"

About half of them said "Well known" and the other half "Yes, indeed". At a less solemn moment I might have found the folk-song effect entertaining. As it was, I could only say, with a dry mouth: "Go on."

"I expect," said Dru, courteously, "that it is ignorance that is at the back of your refusal. It is often so. You do not understand modern methods. You are thinking of the Spanish Inquisition. Yes? And dungeons and racks?" Titter from the first violins. Nothing from me. "And of ingenious Chinese gentlemen who tie their victims beneath a single drop of water which falls upon their foreheads until they go mad. Ha ha."

"Ha ha," said the wind instruments, obediently.

"Put such ideas out of your head. They are old fashioned.

Too slow. Too uncertain. *Too complicated.* They give the victim too much time to be sorry for himself. Once let a man be sorry for himself and he becomes a martyr. A resistance is built up. You see, I am quite frank with you."

Although the Colonel retained his academic manner perfectly, his audience were not so restrained. Some of the younger ones were beginning to dribble already.

"What we aim at nowadays is simplicity, speed, and certainty. Have you ever considered how a performing dog is trained? A hoop is placed in front of him. He does not move. He is touched with a red-hot iron. He moves, through the hoop. A second time. The same thing. Perhaps a third time, too. After all, dogs are not as intelligent as human beings. After that there is no trouble at all. When he sees a hoop he jumps through it. If he does not, he *knows* he will be burnt. It is as simple as that."

I managed a yawn.

The Colonel said, "Quite right. I must not let my enthusiasms run away with me. Now to your case. I think of a question. Something quite simple. What shall it be? Something simple enough to be answered by "Yes" or "No". Let me see. We will take this question. "Is it Lady's intention to provoke a General Strike?""

I hope I preserved my composure. If the roof had fallen on me I could hardly have been more shocked.

I was aware that a cold, piggy eye was gleaming at me.

"All right," I said. "You ask me a question."

"I then give you ten seconds. If you do not answer me in ten seconds I will boil off your right hand."

"You will what?"

"Place it in a saucepan of water and bring it to the boil."

"You—"

"But remember. The essence of this is certainty. You will have only ten seconds to answer, and to answer quite truthfully. After that time, nothing that you say or do will have any effect at all; until the treatment is complete. Then we can start again."

"But—"

M

"Is it Lady's intention to provoke a General Strike?"

There was a clock on the wall with a big second hand. I watched it up to four. Then, for an agonising moment, I thought I had miscounted and I found myself shouting.

"Yes."

"There was no hurry," said Dru. "You had all of ten seconds. Now we will start again. When is the strike to be?"

"I don't know," I said at once. "He wouldn't tell me."

Then we sat in silence as the second hand moved through its allotted span, and I felt the sweat start out all over my body, like water from a wrung cloth.

"Five," said Dru, after what seemed an age. And then "Ten."

"So, he did not tell you. A pity."

One of the telephones on the desk rang discreetly. It must have been a special telephone, because Dru went straight to it, picked it up, and said "Colonel Dru speaking." Then he said, "I see. If you would kindly wait a moment."

He placed his hand over the mouthpiece and said to Major Becker, "Take him away. You know where to put him. I will speak to him again in the morning."

The crowd was melting quietly out of the room. Becker took me professionally holding my arm just above the elbow, and two of the men fell in behind me.

As we went I heard the Colonel say into the telephone. "I was having the room cleared. Now please, if you will go on."

The room had not been particularly hot but as we came out into the passage I felt as if I was coming out of a Turkish bath.

Chapter XIV

IN WHICH I CATCH UP

WE climbed, in all, six flights of stairs. After the third we had to stop for Becker to get his breath back. He was in no sort of condition.

The final flight was narrow, steep and uncarpeted. It ended at the junction of an L-shaped corridor out of each arm of which opened two doors.

We must have been on the top storey of one of the corner turrets (the north-eastern one, I calculated). In the orginal scheme of things the rooms would have served as box-rooms, perhaps, or servants' bedrooms. Now it seemed to be a special sort of prison block.

The original doors had been taken out and much stronger ones put in their place. Doors of planks, pierced by one small square spyhole, and fastened on the outside by two long bolts. We went into the end room.

"I regret," said Becker, with ponderous sarcasm, "it is not luxurious."

I took no notice of the fat Major. After Dru he was just a long drink of water.

The room was bare. Bare wooden floor, bare walls, a single window, a high ceiling, from which swung a single light. In the middle of the floor stood the only piece of furniture, a big, old fashioned bedstead, a bed of the unyielding sort, with plenty of scrollwork and four brass knobs, one at each corner. On it lay a thin and lumpy mattress and one single small, extremely tattered blanket.

"It is an apartment we keep for special guests," said the Major. "Those we are anxious to keep with us. It has every modern convenience—" he indicated the bed—"and plenty of fresh air." He walked over to the window and opened it and stared out pointedly. He seemed to be waiting for me, so I walked across and looked out too.

Eighty feet below us, lighted by arc lamps, was the court-yard. There was something else too. For a moment I could not make it out. Then I saw. Set into the concrete surface of the yard were a number of steel spikes. They were, I think, pieces of angle-iron, which had been cut to an acute point at the top; and they were arranged in a cheval-de-frise immediately under my window.

"We have sometimes found our guests curiously anxious to leave us," said the Major with a smirk. "We might, of course, have fastened up the window, but that would have been contrary, would it not, to all the rules of hygiene? We therefore thought it best to discourage any unorthodox exit. One must admit, of course, that if you were *really* determined, the presence of our little pincushion would not prevent you from throwing yourself out. However, of the fifty or more guests we have entertained, no one has yet made the attempt."

I walked over to the bed, sat down on it, and yawned as rudely as I could.

"Quite right," said the Major, with a sneer. "Quite right. We must not keep you from your bed. The best of dreams. If you are cold, you can always run round the room. Should you need anything, just ring the bell. No one will come."

"Stop behaving like a clown," I said.

He stood for a moment, looking down at me. I thought he was going to hit me, and did not greatly care. Then he said: "Curious that you should be so truculent now. You did not seem to be truculent a short time ago, ha ha! Or was I mistaken?"

I said nothing, and he went out. I heard the bolts shot home and I heard the Major posting one of his men at the far end of the corridor, and giving him some instructions. He was too far off for me to hear what was said to him, but his job was pretty simple. All he had to do was to put himself where he could watch all four doors, and see that none of the prisoners tried to lean out and fiddle with the bolts (which were out of reach, anyway, and fastened home with a patent lock that needed a special key to open it).

I turned out the light, and sat down on the edge of the bed.

It was there that fear got hold of me. It came with the sudden silence. It filtered in with the half-light, from the open window. It laid its fingers upon me and loosed my reins and sinews. At that moment if I had been forced to stand I think my knees would have betrayed me.

Will-power is a tricky thing. It has unimaginable reserves and unexpected limitations. A climber has more occasion to think about it than most people for any difficult climb is a three cornered fight between will, body and the rock face. By hard experience I had found out a certain amount about my own equipment. And one thing I was certain about was that I could not afford to compromise.

Dru had broken me once; and that meant that in future battles, the odds were heavily in his favour.

There were other considerations, but they were of lesser importance. It was becoming clear to me, for instance, that I had been made a fool of. Twice bitten by Lady, I had a third time proffered my hand. He had, of course, concurred in my kidnapping. He may even have known of the exact method and route that were to be used. I do not mean that he had arranged it; that would have been an unnecessary refinement. All he had to ensure was that the guards were posted in the wrong places.

He had allowed me, then, to be kidnapped. So that I might be tortured into revealing the half truths that he had pumped into me. It added insult to injury that he had carefully put me on my guard by explaining to me, in advance, the rules by which he worked.

My mind refused to contemplate just what was going to happen to me when I had been sounded by Dru and his assistants and found to be empty; or what I was likely to suffer in the process.

A cold and comfortless self-contempt had got hold of me. This was the moment of truth, which comes to a climber when he finally realises that he can do no more. He can go neither forward nor back, neither up nor down. Whether he holds on or drops off is between him and his Maker. It concerns no one else in the wide world.

It was my anger with Lady that saved the day. Anger can be as warming as alcohol. And much more permanent in its effects. I sat up, quite suddenly, on that ludicrous iron bedstead, and swore that I would twist Lady's neck for what he had done to me.

I had not until that moment considered my position objectively at all. But now I did two things which in retrospect seem to me significant. I kicked off my shoes and padded across to the door. The guard was sitting on a chair at the end of the passage. He looked about as mobile as the Tower of London. Then I glanced at my watch. It was almost exactly eleven o'clock.

As an abstract problem, what I had to do did not merit any great expenditure of thought. The room I was in was built to hold. It was beyond imagination that I could make any impression on the woodwork of the walls or floor or ceiling. Certainly I could do nothing effective without attracting the instant attention of my guard. He might be resting on the base of his spine, but he wasn't as fast asleep as all that. And anyway, I had no semblance of a tool to cut or hack my way out with. Not a blade, not a pin, not a nail.

Which left the window.

This was not guarded with shutters or bars. My captors had insolently relied an an older and stronger barrier.

(I suppose that a desperate man might have wrought himself up to the pitch where he would have cast himself on the bare stones of the courtyard. But I do not believe that of any man born of woman would deliberately have impaled himself alive on those steel spikes which winked up so hopefully at him from the abyss.)

However, since it was the only way, it was the way I must take. I must plan it with forethought; arrange such aids as I might; and trust to my ability for the rest.

The first problem was direction. To go sideways promised little. If I managed to circle the turret I should merely find myself with my problem repeated on the sheer face of the building. To go down would need eighty foot of reliable rope and the single blanket was so old as to be virtually useless. The cover of the mattress was more hopeful. If I could succeed in tearing it quietly and plaiting it, into strips, it might give me fifteen feet. Which might be enough to reach the window underneath me.

It was the beginning of an idea, and better than nothing. I went across to the window, put my legs through, let them slip down, and then, holding the sill with my right hand, I pushed myself out, until my head and body were clear. A quick look down was enough. The window underneath me, and the one under that, were both shuttered, flush to the sills.

I pulled myself back into the room.

(I was glad to notice, incidentally, that this preliminary exercise had not worried me. Not to be afraid of 'exposure' is one of the first things a climber learns; and in the end a so-called 'head for heights' becomes as much a part of his equipment as his crampons or rope. But like other faculties, it is one that fatigue or hunger, or even the stress of emotion, can easily impair.)

If it was a straight choice between down and up, there was a lot to be said for going up. It was clear that the top of the turret must be above the guttering level of the roof. If, therefore, I proceeded on an upwards diagonal course, I must, quite quickly, strike the spot where the turret joined the roof. This would avoid the difficult 'overhang' caused by the guttering of the turret itself.

Whether or not I could venture on such a course depended almost entirely on the state of preservation of the brickwork. If it had been a new house, or even an old house, with the brickwork recently repointed, it would have been hopeless from the start. I leaned out of the window again and felt with my finger nail.

It was better than I had dared to hope. The mortar between the bricks was comparatively soft and flakey. Moreover the bricks had originally been laid with a wider band of mortar between them than you would find in English building.

I sat down again on the bed. What I proposed was feasible. It was still hideously dangerous.

My plan was to make an ascent, by the use of pitons, or metal pegs, of the diagonal stretch of fifteen foot or so of brick wall which separated my window from the point where the swell of the turret touched the eaves of the main building.

I should need a minimum of seven pegs, each at least ten inches long, strong enough to bear my weight. The ideal would be a standard alpine ice-piton, with a serrated point and a flattened end; an ideal for which I might whistle. In addition I wanted a mallet, heavy enough to drive the pegs, but soft enough not to awaken the guard who was now snoring uneasily on his hard perch.

I turned my attention to the bed. The foot was formed of a single cross bar of cast iron, too thick to break, and too long to be of any use. The head was more promising, and I examined it closely.

It was made in three parts. A centre part of four uprights —fifteen inches long, I judged; flanked on either side by a shorter section of four uprights each rather less than a foot long. Hand me a metal saw, remove the guard, and a quarter of an hour's work would have given me twelve useful pegs.

The centre part seemed to me the most hopeful. It had a double rail at the top. Now if I could lay my hands on a straight, heavy, lever, I could insert it between the two bars, and using the lower one as a fulcrum, could certainly shift the top one. Once the heads were free I could bend those four iron bars out of their sockets at the bottom. The bending, if judiciously performed, would leave each bar with the sort of chisel edge I needed.

If I had a lever.

Any piece of metal, a foot or more long, an inch or two inches thick, and stout enough not to break or bend under pressure.

I kicked my heels at this obstacle for nearly half an hour before I realised that the answer was staring me in the face.

I got up and walked across to the window. It was a perfectly ordinary English type sash window, made in two halves either of which ran up and down on cords in its own wooden slot. And at the end of each cord must hang, I knew, although

I could not see it, exactly the lever I needed; the counter weight of the window.

I fingered the woodwork. It was oldish, and needed paint but it was still quite sound. A chisel, a screwdriver, even a pocket knife, would have been enough to have opened it.

If I had a pocket knife.

At this point the guard showed signs of life, and I sank back as quietly as I could on my bed. When he had had a peep at me, and lumbered back to his seat, and resettled himself, I looked again at my watch.

Half past twelve.

Surely I could find the tiny piece of metal necessary to unlock this ultimate door. The whole bed was made of metal. The base of it was jointed diamonds of thick metal wire. A single one of those would do the trick.

I turned back to the mattress. If I could bend back the tip of one of them, I could soon work it loose. It was too strong for my bare fingers. I needed another piece of metal to start it with. Anything would do. A large coin. A half-crown, even a penny.

If I had a penny.

Quite suddenly I started to laugh. Kneeling beside the bed, I was overcome with the sheer, ludicrous perversity of my position. How did the rhyme go? Water, water quench fire, fire won't burn stick, stick won't beat dog, dog won't bite pig, pig won't get over the stile, and I shan't get home tonight.

When I had finished laughing I examined the bed once more. It occurred to me that something might be done with the brass knobs. I think what put it into my head was that at school we had slept in beds of much this mark, and it had been one of our ploys to unscrew the knobs, and leave notes for each other inside the shank of the post. It occurred to me that if the knob was indeed hollow, it might supply just the edge I wanted.

The first one I tried was stiff, but I could tell that it was made to move, I exerted pressure, and started it. Quietly, quietly. I dared not hurry for fear of making a noise. At

last the knob was clear. I shook it, and a folded spill of paper
fell on to the floor.

With fingers that hardly seemed to belong to me I unfolded the paper. Then I carried it across to the window and
spread it clumsily out on the sill.

It started without preamble:

"I wonder if you will catch up? You are such a devilish
determined person that I believe you will. A slow starter,
Philip, but I've never known anything in this world to
stop you when once you get going. As you will gather,
I'm writing this as my last will and testament. This is
the end of the road. I'm afraid I know something that
Dru will stop at nothing to extract, and I have not got
enough confidence in my powers of detachment to face
him again. Luckily I am equipped to deal with this
situation."

(They must have found the cyanide capsule *after* Colin
had used it. That, of course, was why they had examined
my teeth so carefully).

"It's quite possible that this will all be old news to you.
It may already have reached you by another route. More
by luck than judgment I managed to tip the wink to one
of Schneidermeister's boys. He was on hand when they
unloaded me from the boat. He couldn't help me, but
the word should get back, through their frontier net-
works. I doubt it can be in time to do me any good, but
I hope it may stop someone else dropping down the
same hole.

The main thing, as you have probably guessed, is to
deal with Trüe. You realise that she was selling us all up
the river? I confess it came as a complete shock to me.
But I am not sure that I feel able to judge her. Her father
and mother (did she tell you they were dead?) are very
much alive, and stand surety to her masters for her good
behaviour."

(Yes, I think I had guessed. She had sold her body to me so

coldly that it could not have been for other than adequate consideration.)

"Nothing more to say, Philip, and this pen is running out."

Then a scrawl which might have been "Goodbye" or "Good night."

I refolded the paper, very carefully, and put it into my pocket. Then I picked up the brass knob, inserted its hollow edge behind the wire of the bed spring, and twisted until the wire came loose; bent open the wire and drew it out. Then I went across to the window, fiddled the end of the wire behind the wooden slat, and worked the slat out far enough to get a finger under it. It was only a question of time and patience before I had loosened the wood enough to lift it out. (It was simply held by two short nails, and was, I fancy, left like that for convenience when a sash cord needed mending.)

On reflection, I decided, at the cost of a little extra time and labour, to take out both sides and remove the bottom window bodily. As long as I was fiddling with one side only I was in deadly danger of making some noise that would bring my guard out of his uneasy dreams of beer and sauerkraut.

When I had got both the side-slats out, I raised the bottom window as high as it would go, thus lowering the counter-weights until they rested on the sill. Then I untied the cords and, holding them in one hand, lowered the window again until the cords ran out of the pulleys at the top. Then I lifted the whole window clear and stood it against the wall behind the door. Even if my guard happened to look at the window, I did not think it would have been easy for him to see that one half was gone entirely.

Then I lifted out the left hand sash weight. It was a trifle shorter than I had hoped, a fat, cylindrical pig of lead with a loop at the top for the cord.

Before using it I swathed it carefully with a long strip off my blanket and then inserted the tip between the two top rails of the centre piece of the bed back and pressed gently downwards.

Both bars bent, but neither gave way entirely.

I moved my lever up to one end, and tried again. Flushed with success, I forgot all caution. There was an appallingly loud crack.

I held my breath.

It had sounded like a gun going off. If that didn't wake the guard, he was a good sleeper. I think it did something to his subconscious, for I heard the rattle of a chair down the corridor. Then blessed silence. I gave him a full five minutes to settle back into dreamland before I moved again. Then I found that the results exceded my expectations. The bottom of the two cross bars had broken clean away. The top one was so far bent up that I could draw out all four of the uprights. The middle ones came easily. The two end ones needed more work, but they came finally. I simply took their tops and bent them, one by one, out of their sockets.

I suppose that I assumed that having got so far the other bars would somehow come too. I was wrong. The side portions were independent of the centre and, since they had only one cross bar I was unable to get any purchase for my homemade lever. I tried to bend the bars separately, but they we beyond my strength.

When the sweat ran cold down my face and I found my fingers trembling with the effort I had wasted, I pulled myself up.

It was maddening to be so near and yet so far. Four pegs for fifteen feet. An acrobatic monkey might have made it. Not me. I should need at least seven—preferably nine.

And then I remembered old Rannecker's account of how he had got himself singlehanded out of a crevasse on the Costa Brava. Captive pitons! Could I do it? Dare I do it? Using proper equipment, with rings at the piton ends and nylon rope it was perilous enough. Rannecker did it to save his life, and it was the last time he ever climbed alone. But he had covered sixty feet, shifting his pitons *twelve* times. I had to go fifteen feet and should have to make, perhaps, only three independent moves.

The sweat stood out on me again as I thought of it. A

climb with pitons is a thing outside the experience of the ordinary mountaineer in this country. The placing of an isolated peg might be tolerated in an emergency. That is all. Nevertheless, it *is* quite possible to make a straight climb up a sheer face using pegs all the way. You make it in exactly the same way as a climb with an ice axe. First, you cut grips for right hand and right foot; then, using the grips you have cut, fashion further grips, higher up, for left hand and left foot; and so on, whilst strength and nerve last. When working with pitons the same process is employed, a peg being driven instead of a slot being cut. The effort is the same. The difficulty is simply that you must carry with you sufficient pegs for the whole journey.

And that was where Rannecker's ingenuity came in. He had only four pegs and he had sixty foot to cover. Therefore he attached a length of cord to each peg and dragged the pegs he stood on with him as he went; *using the same pegs over and over again.*

But he was using mountaineering gear. Not soft iron rods broken from a bedstead and lengths of rotten sash cord.

I took another look at my watch, and thought for a moment that my eyes were playing tricks. It was already nearly a quarter to four. If I was going to make the effort I had about an hour in hand. Between half-past four and five would be the ideal time. There would be just enough light to see what I was doing. And perhaps even a kindly early morning mist to seal the eyes of any watchers on the ground.

First I must bend the ends of two of my bars far enough round to take a cord without slipping. This was difficult, but not impossible. I pushed each bar in turn back into the slot and bent it as far as I dared. Then I tore the sash cords out of their grooves in the side of the window, jerking the nails out, carefully, one by one. I had thought, to start with, that I should need to cut them, but it now occurred to me that I only needed to rope the bottom two pitons.

The next question was whether I climbed with shoes or without. There were dangers both ways. The danger of slipping if I kept them on. The dangers of bruising and of cramp if I dispensed with them.

In the end I decided on a compromise. I took out the thick cork undersole from each shoe and put it inside my woollen sock. This gave me a grip and afforded a degree of protection. Incidentally, it also solved the question of the mallet. A heavy shoe, the heel muffled in several thicknesses of blanket, was as good a hammer as I could have devised.

I was well aware that if once I stopped to think I should never go. So I gave myself no chances.

I put the spare shoe into my trouser pocket, tied the ends of the two cords to my wrists, took my home-made pitons in one hand and my shoe in the other, and stepped out on to the window sill.

Chapter XV

TIGER'S ROUTE

THE first moves were easy. All I had to do was to stop thinking about the drop underneath me.

I hammered one peg in at waist height, a couple of foot to the right of the window. It went in easily, but felt nice and firm, nevertheless. The peg was about twelve inches long, and I buried nine inches before I stopped hitting it. The hammering didn't sound too loud, but it was clear that the blanket covering wasn't going to last.

Standing on tiptoe, I then put in the second peg as high as I could above the first. This would have to be done one handed, and I found that the best way was to work the point in for an inch or two, then leave the peg, feel for the shoe which, when not in use, lay inside the front of my shirt, reach up, and hammer the peg home.

(You will understand that as I was standing on the window-sill there was, at the moment, no necessity for such fancy work, but I thought it better to get the drill right whilst I was in a position to experiment.)

Then I stood, for a moment, mapping out the route. The strength of any climb is knowing exactly what you are going to do. One of the additional difficulties here was that the breast of the turret made it impossible to see the point I was aiming for, the junction with the main wall at gutter level. I deduced it must exist because I could, of course, see the main wall, and could judge where the join must come.

I reckoned that I had to make a sideways movement of perhaps twelve foot and an upward climb of a little more. Allowing that my reach was six foot, I had the best part of eight or nine foot to cover before I could scramble on to my objective.

Nine foot up; a little less than nine foot across.

191

In other words, once I was straddled, I had to move all four pegs three times each. That was the sum total. Provided my strength held out, and I didn't get cramp and didn't lose my head or my foothold, or arouse the guard by my knocking or the attention of anyone else by my manœuvres.

The last was the least of the dangers. Being above the arc lights I was in shadow. And an observer, looking up, had the light to contend with.

Thinking was not going to cure any of my other problems.

I put my right foot on one peg, took hold of the other with my right hand, and pulled myself up. I balanced for a moment to get the feel of it. The piton was too thin, and bit into my foot through the cork sole. Nevertheless, it felt firm. If they all went as well as that, I could do it.

Using my left hand I drove in my two other pegs, one at waist height, the other above my head.

Then I transferred my weight to my left foot, and steadying myself with my left hand, stepped up.

Now for the pay-off. I gripped the cord firmly in my right hand, bent down as far as I dared, and pulled. The peg slewed towards me and stuck. I gave a little jerk in the opposite direction, like an awkward angler casting against the stream. Then back again. Once, twice, three times, and it was out.

Mixed with my triumph was a much colder feeling.

I was under no misapprehension as to what I had done. The way back was now sealed. I could pull the peg out by its cord all right but no contortion I could devise would get me into a position to hammer it back again.

I could only go up. Sideways and upwards.

The first two moves went with suspicious smoothness. I realised that the actual physical effort was not going to be the limiting factor; not at that point, anyway. Accidents apart, it seemed that it would be a question of whether I could reach the roof before I was crippled by cramp in my legs or the soft but repeated hammering brought my guard running into the room.

(The thought of what he would say, or do, almost made me laugh for the second time that night.)

It was the next move which started the trouble. I found the greatest difficulty in getting the peg in at all. I was well balanced, on my left foot and was using my right hand for hammering so there ought to have been no difficulty.

It occurred to me that I might have chosen an unlucky place. With great caution I pulled the peg clear, and tried again, one brick lower. It was a little better, but not much. It took a deal of uncomfortably noisy hammering to get the peg home.

In the end it was done; and I shifted my position for the third time.

At this point all my doubts became certainties. For some reason or other as I got higher, the mortar was getting harder. Possibly it was because I was now coming under the area sheltered by the overhang of the roof, and for this reason the wall face had suffered less from the weather.

This time I had to use my hammer left-handed. The results were unencouraging. The foot peg went in to about half its length, and there it stuck. The more I hit it the looser it became. The peg for my hand went in less than that.

I had cut my slender margin of safety in half.

Stop for a minute, and think it out.

This was the moment at which, in any normal climb, I should have turned back. But I could not turn back. I could only go on. I must accept a non-existent margin of safety because I had no choice. But there was another reason too. A purely psychological one. I could now see my goal. My progress had brought me far enough round the curve of the turret to see the point at which I was aiming.

Above my head, and about five foot to my right was the point where the main guttering touched the circumference of the turret. And, to make the sight even more tempting, there was a down drainage pipe in the angle of the wall (If I had been thinking properly I should have deduced that there must be).

If only I could now have gone *downwards* and sideways all

N

would have been well. For I could have descended, crab-wise, into an area of softer mortar until I reached the drain pipe, and then climbed up it onto the roof. But by no power on earth could I descend. By no contortion could I drive in a piton at lower than knee level.

It was maddening to realise how near I had come to success. My calculations seemed crazy yet in the event they had proved absolutely correct. But for the successive hardening of the mortar, I should only have had to make two more, comparatively easy, steps and I should have been safe on that roof.

Fear is a bad counsellor to a climber; but anger may be worse.

I gave each of those shaky pegs a final tap for luck, gripped the top one and stepped onto the lower.

Almost at once the lower peg started to bend under my weight.

I increased the grip of my hand. Previously I had been using the upper peg lightly, to maintain balance. Now I was actually suspended from it.

Which introduced a final, limiting, factor. The length of time I could support myself by the strength of one hand, for my foothold was sloped out to such a degree that it was almost useless.

With a cold feeling of desperation, I pulled out the free hand peg, moved it across and up as far as I dare, and drove it in. By the mercy of God, I had struck a moderate patch and it went in a certain way.

The lifting and driving of the bottom peg was the hardest work I have ever tried in my life. My left foot had now almost no grip at all and my left wrist was weakening dangerously. Again I struck a fair patch, and it was this alone that saved me. Six blows brought the peg home.

I pulled on my left wrist, got my toe onto the right peg, lifted, got my new hand hold, and, in that instant, lost my left peg.

How it happened I have no clear idea. I had been almost hanging on it and I can only think that the sudden removal of my weight jerked it. It slipped from my fingers, and seconds later, I heard the pretty tinkle as it landed on the courtyard.

(I fell with the peg; turning over and over in the air. All my calculations had been false. I had thought I was far enough over to avoid the spikes. I must have been wrong, for one of the spikes went right through me. It was curious that I felt no pain.)

At what interval of time after this I do not know, but a matter of seconds only, I guess, my head cleared, and I found that I was staring stupidly at my left hand.

I was still standing, with my right foot firmly on its peg and my right hand holding fast. But there was something wrong with left wrist. The cord had gone. In grabbing at the hand peg, the loop over my wrist must have slipped.

Quite slowly I looked down. The foot peg was still in the wall. The cord was trailing from it. And it was as effectively out of my reach as the hand peg which had just fallen eighty foot into the courtyard.

I was stranded, balanced on one shaky spike, holding on to another, and three foot from my goal.

How long it took me to work out the last step I have no idea. Time had ceased to have much meaning.

Then I saw the solution.

The first thing was to change hands and feet. The hand was easy enough. The foot was another matter; but I did it with a sort of awkward shuffle. I was beyond caring for finesse.

Then, taking as firm a grip as I could with my left hand, I threw myself across to the right, hand and right foot together.

My fingers scrabbled for a moment, then found the top of the pipe.

Seconds later I was on the roof. I threw myself forward, flat, my right cheek against the dew-wet slates, and lay for five minutes without stirring, savouring what it was like to be alive again.

It was the sound of a car that stirred me. It was coming along the main road at the foot of the wooded knoll on which my prison house stood. I could see the head lights, but they were dimmed by the light of morning, which was coming up with strides.

In ten minutes the sun would be up.

I must move. And I must face the next decision, which was likely to be a difficult one.

The house was built in a hollow square round a central courtyard, with a turret at each corner joined by a long stretch of shallow pitched, slated, roof. Moving along the roof presented no difficulty. Feeling myself a little conspicuous on the outer perimeter, I clambered, flat-footed, up the ridge of the two roofs behind my turret and slid down the gully on the inner side. All my movements were slow and heavy. I was suffering from the most desperate reaction and was, besides, physically finished.

On the inner lip of the roof, overlooking the courtyard, I found a lead-lined cat-walk which served as a gutter or as a footway, I supposed, for workmen on the roof. I saw that by keeping to it I could make a complete detour of the building. It was broken by the dormers of half a dozen windows in each side of the square but these were shallow affairs, which I could scramble over as I came to them.

I was now out of sight of anyone on the ground, and I sat down to try and think.

As I sat, the sun came over the horizon in the pink glory which means wet weather, and sounds of returning life came clearly to my ears, funnelled up to me from the inner court below. A door slammed. A tin pail was clanked down on a hard floor. And a man began to whistle, sadly out of tune.

The moment for decision had come.

There was no doubt in my own mind that I could break in through one of the dormer windows. My faithful cord was still round my right wrist, and from it dangled my last remaining piton. With it I could quickly force the window latch and get back into the building. Supposing the door to be open I could then make my way to the ground and try to get out. That was where my imagination stopped working. I was certain to run into trouble. Trouble which I was too weary either to avoid or to fight. And if, by a miracle, I did get clear of the house without being seen, what then? I should be in the grounds, presumably guarded, of a Police Head-quarters in full daylight.

I knew what the alternative was, but the truth of the matter is that I was afraid of it. Having got so far, I wanted to get further still. I wanted to get clear of that hellish building and out into the kindly countryside.

It was the same instinct that has made many an escaping prisoner of war rush the frontier at the end of a night's march when his legs were too weak even to carry him over it. I had just enough sense to resist it.

I broke open the nearest window. No finesse was required here. I used the heel of my shoe to break the glass and thrust my hand through and slipped the catch. I was in an empty attic. The door opened on to a corridor.

I left that door open.

Then I went back to the window and climbed out on to the leadwork again.

From this point I took care to leave no trace of my progress. I moved carefully and slowly, avoiding the occasional puddle and drift of sodden leaves, until I had made my way round two complete sides of the square. I was now diametrically opposite the point at which I had made my ascent.

Starting from here. I peered into each dormer window in turn. I wanted to find a room with stuff stored in it. Since, if there was stuff in the room, it was likely to have a locked door.

The first two rooms were empty. The third, which seemed to be some sort of store room, was more hopeful. I slipped the end of my faithful piton under the catch and eased it open; stepped in, and closed and latched the window behind me.

The jumble of stuff almost filled the room. There were dusty hangings, roughly folded and piled together. Some of the largest fire-irons I have ever seen, thick with rust. Two or three tea chests, which were locked. A dozen or more chairs of the comfortless concert-room variety; a canvas back-drop on struts of a "castle battlement with one practical entrance up-prompt"; some religious bannerets, and an enormous, papier mâché frog's head. I burrowed carefully in behind a pile of hangings. My bed was dusty and cramped, but I could have slept on spikes in Little Ease.

When I came round again I had a throat like a kiln and a nagging headache; and my arms and legs felt as if they had been on the rack. Also, in spite of the warmth of my dusty coffin, I was shivering. I extricated myself and moved cautiously over to the window.

It was nearly eight o'clock. I had been out of the world for thirteen hours, and the sun had swung in its orbit from East to West, and the World had moved one day nearer the moment of its final dissolution, whereafter it would circle for ever, a desolate cinder in a forgotten planetary system.

And how had they all passed the day? Lady and the General. Gheorge, Lisa and Trüe. And how was Colonel Dru feeling?

No doubt my defection had been reported to him.

An arc light came on in the courtyard and I shrank back from the window. But it was not aimed at me. It was directed downwards. Something was happening in the courtyard, and since anything that went on in that building could be my concern, I craned to look.

Four men had marched out. They were in the uniform of the Jagd-Polizei the Hunting Police; and they carried rifles.

Then two more men appeared. They had someone by the arms. Someone in shirt sleeves and open neck. Someone I thought I recognised.

A chair was fetched, and the shirt-sleeved man slumped in it. As he was being tied to it, I recognised him. It was my sentry of the night before.

Four rifles sounded together. The man in the chair jumped as if hot needles had been stuck into him; strained for a minute and then sagged into a parody of sleep. He had been a great sleeper. Reveille would trouble him no longer.

The men filed off. The lights went out. That scene was over.

Before it got too dark to see I tackled the door of the room. I wasn't worried about it, because I knew that, at a pinch, I

could always get out of my window and move along until I
found a room with an open door. But this one gave me no
trouble. It was designed to keep people from outside getting
in. In the end I loosened one of the screws which held the
keeper of the lock, and twisted the whole keeper back until
it was clear of the tongue.

Then I waited. If anyone came in at the door I would put
on the papier mâché head and recite the Frogs' Chorus from
Aristophanes. That should give them something to think
about.

I must then have gone to sleep again, sitting, for the next
thing I remember is looking at my watch and seeing that the
time was eleven o'clock.

Almost exactly forty-eight hours ago I had said to Trüe:
"What do I do now?" and the little witch had said to me:
"Just walk out of the exit and take a look at the booths."

Oh, the sweet child.

I creaked to my feet, an old, old man, and walked across
to the door and opened it. Everything was quiet up on the
top storey, but there was plenty of life below.

I turned up the collar of my coat and buttoned it across to
hide my shirt. And I wound the cord round one end of faithful old peg to form a grip. Piton, jemmy, and now life-
preserver. A versatile piece of iron.

On the third floor I found a bathroom with the door open,
and went in and drank a gallon of water and felt a bit better.

Then I ventured down another storey.

Clearly it would be a lot safer not to use the ground floor
at all. There was certain to be some sort of night staff in
charge.

Better to try one of the rooms on the first storey. Best of
all, if I could get into the one next to the turret where there
should be a down pipe corresponding to the one I had
reached the roof by. Anyway, I ought to be able to drop from
a first storey window.

Unless they had spikes all round the house.

The first storey passage was carpeted. I located the bathroom, but the window was too small, and opened only at

the top. Next door should be a bedroom. I opened the door and looked in. Someone gave a strangled grunt and said: "Who the Hell's that?" I shut the door, and retreated round the angle of the stairs.

I heard the bedroom door open and someone breathing heavily. Then the door shut. That's all right, old chap. Just the fairies paying you a visit.

I went on up to the floor above and eased open the door of the room above the one I had just visited. This one was empty and looked unused. I opened the window. And there was the hoped-for down-pipe. It looked stout, and had thoughtfully been set away from the wall so that I could get my fingers round it. Just what the burglar ordered. I took off my shoes and dropped them down the front of my shirt, swung out, and started slowly down the pipe.

The window under me was tightly shut. Evidently the grunter had heard about the dangerous properties of fresh air. I felt an urge to rap on his window, but refrained. A minute later I was sitting on the ground putting my shoes on.

The South was the deserted side of the building. Ahead of me was a slope, thickly covered with trees and bushes, a line of lights, and freedom.

I scuttled across the path and got under cover. The going was not too bad. It was a formal garden which had been deliberately allowed to run riot. The rambler roses were the main difficulty, although there was a sort of giant yucca which had to be treated with respect.

There was plenty of time, and I moved forward with great caution. One thing I had in mind was the possibility of trip-wires; but if any were there, luck took me past them. Ten minutes brought me to the lights. They were a line of overhead electric lights, on standards, of the sort used in prison camps.

There was also, as I saw by the light of the lamps, a very formidable fence. This was prison camp standard, too. First a fence of single strands, taut and close together and topped by an additional section bent back at such a sharp reverse angle as to make climbing almost impossible. Behind that a second similar fence with the top leaning the other way. In between them, bundles and rolls and sheaves of loose barbed wire.

I sat in a giant coreopsis and contemplated it sourly.

The technique for dealing with such an obstacle, as I knew, was to attack it from underneath. Prisoners (working sometimes with foolhardy courage under the very eyes of their guards) would lie, in the shadow, alongside such a fence, snipping a strand here and there, and propping up the loose wire on small forked sticks, until a tunnel had been made through which an agile man might worm his way to freedom.

I had no guards watching me. But, equally, I had no wire cutters.

Given long enough undisturbed there was a chance that I might tunnel underneath the bottom strand; then use the forked stick technique to get through the middle part; and finally dig my way under the outer fence. One more use for my hard-worked piton. The soil looked loose and easy.

And so it proved, for the first six inches. Then I struck the concrete.

I retired to my coreopsis. I was conscious of anger and frustration. To have got so far and then to be held up. It was the feeling I had had as I stood, poised ballet-like on one toe, eighty feet above Dru's pincushion. I wanted to attack that fence with my bare hands. Before I could do anything silly, I heard the guard coming and retreated fast. He was a young man, and looked pretty alert. There's nothing like shooting a sentry from time to time to keep people on their toes.

He came slowly past, his eyes on the fence. For a terrible moment I thought he was going to see the mess I had made with my digging. The moment hung, stretched, broke. Then he passed on.

I was already on my way back. The house seemed safer than the garden.

Keeping under cover, I made my way round towards the North West corner. It was here that most of the activity seemed to be centred.

A gravelled drive ran up to a paved courtyard. There were two cars standing in the courtyard, and I looked at them covetously; but the doors and windows were all shut and I suspected that they were locked. Also, there was ten yards of lighted courtyard to cross, right under the eye of the main entrance.

As I watched a third car drove up. The driver seemed to have a grudge against his gear box, and was in a hurry, or a bad temper, or both. In fact, there was an air of activity and urgency about the whole place. Lights on in most of the ground floor rooms, and people coming and going inside the building.

Look at this! He hasn't locked his car. He hasn't even removed the ingnition key. In too much of a hurry. *And* he's parked it on my side of the courtyard. *And* I could turn it in one straight sweep, without backing.

The thought was no sooner in my head than I was in the driving seat.

The engine was still warm. Switch on. One touch of the starter, slam her into gear, and get going.

The guard on the inner courtyard was just shutting the gate. He's seen me come in, in a hurry, a minute before. Now he's going to see me going out again. He just got the gate open again in time, and I caught a glimpse of him in my driving mirror standing under the light, staring after me, his mouth open.

I was on a short, steep, gravelled driveway, with a twist in it. Ahead of me, at the bottom of the hill, hidden for the moment by the bend, was another line of lights. And, no doubt another gate.

Suppose it was shut? Drive straight through it, boy. Hit anything hard enough and it'll go down.

I swung round the bend. The gate was not shut. On the contrary, it had just been opened to admit another car; which was half filling the open space. In the other half was standing Colonel Dru. He had got out of his car to talk to the guard.

I aimed at him with great precision; he spoiled things a

little by moving at the last moment, so that it was only my left side head lamp that hit him, and the left hand front wheel that went over him.

The great car rose for a moment, like a tug on the crest of an oily wave, then came to earth again with a jerk all four wheels scuttering in the dust, as we went on our way.

Hit anything hard enough, and down it goes.

Chapter XVI

FOLLOW-MY-LEADER

As I bowled down that road between the pine trees, the darkness on either side of my headlamps expanding and contracting in an alarming manner, I tried to marshal my thoughts. It wasn't easy. The fact is I was over-driven. I had eaten nothing for more than thirty six hours, and was already in the sharp grip of fever. I had the stars to steer by. The Austrian-Jugo-Slav frontier line lay due west, and I had a very limited time to make the most of the enormous slice of fortune that had dropped into my lap.

Expressions such as "Sealing all exits" and "Warning all posts" flashed into my mind and I tried to consider them dispassionately. How quickly, in fact, could road blocks be set up around a given area? First of all they would have to pick up what was left of Colonel Dru; then the guards would have to telephone the headquarters; and a plan would have to be made; and instructions sent out. It was not as if they were expecting anything of the sort to happen.

I decided that I had at least half an hour in hand. Very probably more. I looked at my watch. It was ten past one. Say I had been going for ten minutes. I then glanced casually at the speedometer and noticed that it registered ninety. Kilometres, not miles, but it was a lot too fast for a blindish road, at night and I eased my foot on the accelerator.

The frontier would lie between twenty and thirty miles away. Clearly I could not drive right up to it. But with any luck I could break the back of the journey.

Road fork. Locate Orion. Fork right.

Twenty minutes.

Scattered light ahead. A village. No, a town. Steady, boy. This is one of the places you don't want to go through. Even if there's no one briefed to stop you. Towns have ears.

I brought the car down to a crawl, and turned out the head-lamps. We were already in the outskirts. A road lined with tall, solid houses set back in their gardens; just like the Banbury road where it runs into Oxford.

What I wanted was a turning. Not just something that was going to lead me a dance through the residential quarter and back into the main road again, but a real turning, that turned. Preferably to the right, for in that direction lay the frontier.

It was whilst I was worrying about this that the petrol gave out. The car gave a warning cough. I looked at the guage, and the next minute there I was, coasting slowly down the road, with nothing behind me but the power of my own momentum.

Luckily we were on a gentle slope. On my left I saw an open drive way, swung across the crown of the road, and put the car in. We made perhaps ten yards before we crunched to a final stop. Around me the silence was complete. Such noises as there were came from inside my own head.

It was only when I got out, that I realised just how shaky my legs were.

I tottered back to the entrance. It was a Private Sana-torium. Doktor Coloris. Pathology and Remedial Exercises. Quite so. Since my car was blocking the Doctor's front drive I could only hope they didn't get up too early at the Sana-torium.

My legs came back to me a little with use. I recrossed the main road, took the first turning to the right, and set my course westward. It took an infinity of time to shake off that town. First the big houses gave way to small houses. Then the small houses degenerated into shacks and bungalows. And finally, at about the turn of the century, I struck the allotment belt.

Don't stop now. All you've got to do is lift one foot and put it down. Then lift the other one and put it down in front of the first. If you do it long enough it gets you somewhere in the end.

As I dragged myself up on to the shoulder of the hill, out

of the town, up into the woods and fields, a breeze began to blow against my hot face. It was the little, old, cold wind that heralds the dawn.

Most of the time, Colin was walking with me. I could hear his voice, bland and reassuring, just behind my left shoulder.

"The Shah, of course, has a personal distrust for the Kaiser." Of course, of course. "The Kaiser, despite their comparable family background, has little use for the King of Spain."

When I got to the top of the ridge, and the down slope started helping my legs, I started on another instalment of thinking.

Ahead of me lay the frontier. In the growing light I could see that same line of hills that I had looked on, in reverse, from the ramparts of Obersteinbruck. It seemed attractively near and I could get up to it, if my legs would keep on working.

And once I got there, I should be recaptured. In my present condition if a girl guide jumped out and said Boo to me I should fall flat on my back.

When I got over the crown of the ridge, I saw that attaining the frontier line was not going to be as easy as it had looked.

About a mile ahead of me, hidden before by the swell of the ground, was a broad cleft. Occupying the cleft were a river, a railway line, and enough houses to make a long village or a short town.

My legs carried me a hundred yards or so closer before my mind ordered me to stop, and I sat down on a rock.

This was no place for me. Lights were coming up in the windows, an engine was shunting on the line, and, even as I watched, some hooter began to blow.

The sound seemed to blow a small measure of sanity back into me.

What I had to do was to get back into the open country behind me and lie up for the day. At the same time, since any search must start from the car, the greater distance I put between it and me the better. My best course would be to go along my side of the valley, until I was clear of the town ahead of me, and there find shelter.

I wanted a lateral path, and after a short cast I found one going in the right direction. Perhaps I ought to have been warned by the fact that it was going down hill. For ten minutes later I turned a corner and the path became a road-way among houses.

And there was at least one man in the roadway.

I swung quickly to my left, saw an opening, and went up it, It was a steep place, with rock steps cut in a clay gulley; probably a spate of water ran down it in the winter months. I turned the bend, and squatted down, my heart bumping.

I heard the man pass by the entrance, and move on up the road. His pace was unhurried and I guessed he had not seen me.

The gulley was too public for me to think of stopping in it. I prayed it might lead me out on to the hillside.

I went up it slowly. At the top it opened out, on to a small plateau, on which stood a square, stone building. What I was in was a short cut or back entrance to this building.

The main road continued on round the side of the hill and served the front of the house which looked like a farm house. No it wasn't. It was a shop. There was a board, with something written on it.

I crawled closer and read "Josef Radk. Importer of and Dealer in Fine Wines" and in smaller letters, underneath, was something which brought the blood to my face "Agency Schneidermeister."

It was an outside chance, but any chance was better than the certainty of discovery. My legs would take me no further. And if I sat where I was, the first village child using the path as a short cut to school would fall over me.

I scrambled up, and shambled across the open space in front of the house. The front door was open, and I fell through it.

Sitting on a high stool, at a desk littered with papers, a cup of coffee in one hand and a pen in the other, was a man.

He looked up quickly as I came in, put down his cup, and said: "You look as if you have come far and fast."

I had an impression of a square white face and of steel-rimmed glasses, behind which lived a pair of watchful eyes. His manner was reserved, but I noticed that he did not seem unduly surprised or alarmed by my irruption into his counting-house.

"Yes," I said. "I have come far and fast. Not that I am unused to travelling. A recent journey with young Franz Schneidermeister—"

"Ah, yes," he said. "You know Franz. Might I suggest that you sit."

He pushed a chair quickly under me and I folded into it. Waves of fatigue were billowing up round me like smoke clouds, and the fever was playing tricks with my eyes. I heard a clinking behind me and a glass was pushed into my hand.

"Drink it," said the man sharply. "All of it. Don't play with it." It was schnapps, half a tumbler of it.

"Now," said the man, "tell me no more than I must know if I am to help you."

I said, "I got away last night from Police Headquarters. I don't know exactly when it was. I stole a car and drove for about fifteen miles. Then I left it, in a town."

"How far away?"

"Hard to say. Perhaps four or five miles. It is over the crest, and in the next valley."

"Feuering, yes."

"Then I walked."

"Who has seen you?"

"So far as I know, no one."

"You are English?"

"Yes."

"Your name?"

I told him.

"I thought it might be you. How is Lisa?"

"Miss Prinz," I said, "was quite well when I saw her last."

I tried to think about Lisa and was alarmed to find that I could not see her face. As I tried desperately to focus her, she turned into Henry, sitting, foursquare, on one of the terrace seats at Twickenham.

And they were playing now. The stands were packed from floor to roof. There go the forwards, working the ball down the field, a check, then out, scrum half to centre, centre to wing, streaking for the line, the crowd roaring; rising as one man and roaring, roaring.

My next clear memories are of the pinpoint flashes from a torch, coming and going between long ages of blackness; blackness in which my mind wandered free, mostly traversing the past few weeks of my life; sometimes I woke for a moment at the sound of a scream, realised that I was listening to my own voice, and dropped back again into the hinterland of illusion. Then there was the taste of soup, which I drank from time to time; and over all, pervading the darkness, assaulting my eyes and ears and nose until it became so much part of the background that I came to accept it, the sour smell of the lees of wine.

On the third night my fever left me, and some time after that I awoke to full consciousness of my surroundings.

I was lying on a pallet bed, swathed in a cocoon of blankets. The floor under me was packed earth, and the wall, a few inches from my left side, was brick.

The darkness was almost complete, but using my fingertips I made out, more or less, that I was lying under the actual staging which supported two or three huge wine barrels. The left side and foot of my bedroom were the rough cellar wall, the right hand side was the wooden staging. I felt backwards behind my head, and in doing so touched a pitcher which held, as I found when I tasted it, a weak mixture of wine and water. I gulped down a mouthful and went to sleep again.

Next time I woke there were several lights showing, and one of the barrels was being shifted. The steel spectacles of Radk gleamed round at me, and his voice from the darkness said: "Lie still, we are moving you to more comfortable quarters."

Hands seized both ends of my pallet bed, and it was lifted.

"I expect I can walk," I said.

"I doubt it," said Radk. "In any event it will be quicker to carry you."

o

It wasn't a private suite at the Dorchester, but it was a nice, clean little room in the attic, and there, that evening, Radk came to talk to me.

"We have been able to bring you out," he said, "because the search has passed on. The police have been here twice in the last five days. Not to ransack us, you understand, but on routine searches. The strength of the ripples, out here on the circumference, suggest that you must have dropped quite a large stone into the centre of the pool," and he looked at me owlishly through his glasses.

"Five days," I said. "How long have I been here altogether?"

"Today is the seventh day."

"How soon can I move?"

"It was only, I think, the fever of exhaustion. You should recover now quite quickly. If you get about and use your legs a little tomorrow and more the following day, you should be strong enough to make the frontier on the third day. It is only five miles. But we must see how you go. Have you reason for haste?"

"I was thinking of you," I said, lamely. "I don't want to get you into trouble now—"

But I lied. It was the hellish country that I was in a fret to be clear of.

"As I was about to say, there should be no difficulty in reaching the frontier. Whether you could cross it at this moment." He shook his head.

"Is it so difficult?"

"Normally of course not. But now! I forget that you have been out of the world for so long."

He went away, and came back with a handful of newspapers.

There was a good deal in them that I found interesting. The first item which caught my eye was an account of the funeral of Colonel Allesandro Dru. It appeared that he had died in a motor accident. Swerving to avoid a child his car had left the road and struck a telegraph post. Szormeny had attended the funeral in person.

Promotion for Major Becker.

But this was small beer. It was the happenings on the political front page that took the eye.

At first, the references were guarded. Labour unrest had occurred in isolated centres due to dissatisfaction over differentials. Heavy Industry and Transportation were chiefly affected. The police had made a number of arrests of agitators and the situation was in hand.

Like hell it was in hand! The headlines grew thicker as the storm gathered.

Two days later the word "General Strike" was first mentioned and prominence was given to a pronouncement by Szormeny.

"I shall not disguise from you," he said in black type, "that the situation is grave. It is by no means desperate, and, if all do their duty, this latest attempt to throttle our economy and disrupt our régime will fail, as earlier attempts have failed. I myself have taken personal charge, during the crisis, of the essential supplies. Coal, electricity and water undertakings. And of all goods and passenger transport. There is not the least cause for alarm. Hoarding will be punished. My message to you all is—defeat this attempt by continuing to live your normal lives."

There was a heavy, competent, common-sense ring about this announcement which I found disquieting. Could a strike ever make headway against a state-in-arms?

However, I could not help noticing that whilst urging his compatriots not to take any alarmist precautions, David Szormeny was not practising all that he preached. A very small item caught my eye. It said "Madame Szormeny, with her two children, has moved from her home in the Eastern Provinces to be near her husband, who is at his post of action in the west. In times like the present, she told our representative, a wife's place is near her husband."

Radk came in at this moment, and I said, "How much have the papers got?"

"About half the truth," he said. "It started slowly, but yesterday, at Kaposvar, men were ordered to take out certain trains and refused. The leaders were shot. That stiffened the resistance."

"Can it succeed?"

"Of course it cannot succeed." He sounded cross. "There is a division of infantry in Kaposvar already. If necessary they will add tanks, guns, aeroplanes. How can it succeed?"

"Perhaps it has succeeded already."

Radk looked at me sharply, as if he suspected a good deal more meaning than I had intended.

"The mere fact of a strike," I explained. "The fact that the authorities have not been able to conceal it from their own people and from western observers. I should call that a victory."

"Oh, certainly," said Radk. "Certainly." He added, "A friend of yours reached Pecs yesterday."

"A friend? Do you mean Lady?"

"The same. He has his courage, that one."

Of a sudden I felt a fever to be gone.

"The frontier was never more difficult," said Radk gloomily. "You will need your legs and your arms, and your wits. You should sleep now."

No doubt I needed sleep. But it was long before I attained it. My mind was in turmoil.

Next day the papers were ominously quiet, but Radk, who seemed well informed, told me that the centre of resistance had moved south to Pecs. I spent the day eating and drinking and doing Mullers exercises on the attic floor to try and get some strength back into my legs and arms.

The next day Radk had some reassuring news for me. "The watch on this frontier has slackened," he said. "One of our men got through last night. I think the truth is that the people they wanted to keep out are all inside Hungary by now. Attention has shifted south with them. You could try your luck tonight, if you wished."

For an hour that evening he instructed me in the ways of the 'passeur.'

"You cannot go directly into Austria," he said. "The country is altogether too flat, and too open. And since it is the obvious way, it is closely guarded. But I will take you on the back of my motor-cycle. Here, you see, on this map. We pass between Pecica and Nadlac and I drop you about— there."

After that he made me memorise the route, until I came to a place called, in Hungarian, the Valley of Twists and Turns.

"It is a strange place," he said. "Twisting sharply, as its name implies, and very steep, like the course of some ancient river. Only there is no water at the bottom. Simply fine white sand. You will know it at once when you see it. Beyond is broken ground, with good cover, rising steeply. The actual frontier line is a mile on, and almost unmarked. The guards are all on the valley, but it is a very difficult place to watch. That is why we choose it for crossings."

"The Jugo-Slav frontier?"

"Yes. You will be touching the extreme north-eastern tip of Jugo-Slavia. It is quite deserted. There is a cabin, which you will reach after an hour's further climb—"

"It also is deserted," I said.

"So. You knew Thugutt?"

"I found him," I said. "And his wife and child."

That was the last talk I can remember with Radk. He took me, by back ways, that evening after dark, to the place he had indicated on the map. He was a brave, cheerful little man, who looked more like a family grocer than a smuggler or a conspirator. I believe he was caught out and shot soon afterwards.

There was a quarter moon, and the night was clear and still, a fact which both helped and hindered. The first part of the journey I took easily, using a little compass Radk have given me. And counting my paces as a rough check on distance.

By midnight I was comfortably settled in a thicket of broom overlooking the Valley of Twists and Turns. It was an eerie place. The moonlight picked out the thread of white sand at the valley bottom, so that it was hard to realise that it was not a river.

The night wind had got up and was moving the leaves and bushes and walking amongst the dried grasses. I gave myself a full hour, and I neither heard nor saw any sign of a human being.

I found this more than a little disturbing. The shining silver ribbon ahead of me was the actual frontier; not the geographical line, but the one on which authority had put its veto and set its watch. And I have never yet met a frontier guard who could hold himself still for an hour. My plans were upset.

I had foreseen myself locating the post on either side of me, timing the movements of the watchers and slipping between them. But there was an unexplained gap. Something which I could not understand and at once suspected.

After tormenting myself with possibilities for a further ten minutes, I moved forward again. The lie of the rocks was forcing me into a used track. I felt like a mouse, treading the first mazes of some elaborate mechanical trap.

From rock to rock, from shadow to shadow. With painful slowness I reached the bottom of the ravine. Sooner or later, now, I must come out into the open. As I gathered myself for the dash I noticed, on the track beside me, and more clearly on the sand ahead of me, a confused trail of footsteps.

A number of other people, perhaps five or six of them, had passed that way, and recently.

If it was a patrol it was a very odd one, for at least one of the shoe-prints had been made by a woman.

Before I had done thinking about it I was across, and going fast up the other side of the valley. The gates of the fortress had been raised, for some purpose that I could hardly define, and it was up to me to squeeze through before they came down again.

Only when my legs started to remind me that I was a convalescent did I drop into shelter.

Not a shout, not a shot. Nothing but my own heaving lungs and pumping heart, and, as these quieted, the ordinary noises of the night.

After a short rest I went on, regulating my pace to conserve my strength. It took me more than the hour that Radk had predicted to reach Thugutt's homestead. The plateau looked creepy enough in the moonlight, but so far as I was concerned it held only kindly ghosts.

Authority had sealed the doors and windows of the cabin, but the grave at the edge of the tree was, so far as I could tell, undisturbed.

More than once, in the next two hours, I had a feeling that there were people moving, at a distance from me, but going in my direction. The wind had dropped, and the night was still; but listen as I would I could never be quite certain. Hearing plays odd tricks up in the hills. Once I thought I heard the sharp clink of iron on stone and could hardly tell whether it came from behind me or in front.

I felt no fears of the railway tunnel. It was the easiest part of the journey.

As I came out at the other side and plunged down the hill, dawn was coming up. It was not, as I had seen it come before, a red line in the east, for light clouds lay across the sky, and there was a heavy mist in all the hollows, but the birds weren't fooled. Like me, they knew it was going to be a lovely day.

I had forgotten that such a thing as fatigue existed; and I might have broken my leg half a dozen times as I cascaded down that slope, with the wind in my face, the birds singing like glory and the light growing every minute.

By my watch it was six o'clock when I reached the track, and ten more minutes brought me to the walls of Obersteinbruck.

The main gate was wide open, but there was no sound of anyone stirring. All asleep, or all gone?

I pushed up the cobbled ramp into the courtyard.

Standing at the front doorway, his hands in the pockets of his old service greatcoat, was Major Piper.

Chapter XVII

"TURNS AGAIN HOME"

WHEN he saw me the Major blinked twice, which I took to be a sign of grave emotion.

"Glad to see you," he said. "I had some news three days ago that suggested you might be back with us soon."

"Where's Lady?"

"We last heard of him at Pecs. He had a good day on Tuesday. The men derailed two engines across the track, and no traffic got in or out. It can't last, of course."

I remember feeling surprised. I suppose it had been at the back of my mind that it was Lady and his party who had passed ahead of me during the night.

"Will he ever get out?"

"It's a difficult question to answer. To my mind a strike's an easier thing to start than it is to stop. As long as there's any life in it Lady won't run away. That's my guess. The trouble is Gheorge and Lisa insisted on going with him."

"And the General?"

"He's returned to the Hague. He's in charge of the section now. I expect the routine work's piled up a bit whilst they've been away. That's the trouble with an office: Things go on piling up."

The question had to be asked some time.

"What about Trüe?"

"Trüe?" said the Major. He seemed to be speaking of someone in the remote past. "Oh, Miss Kethely. Yes. I fancy they cleaned up before they left."

His eye wandered towards the greenwood that carpeted the slope behind the castle; and I knew then that in some hidden glade the busy ants and the wood-lice were making their last bargains with her beautiful, often-sold body.

"I believe they had to put the dogs down. They got out

of hand after she had gone. They were very attached to her, you know."

"They weren't the only ones," I said.

The Major seemed disinclined to dwell on the subject.

"I suppose you had quite an easy passage last night," he said.

"Surprisingly so. It made me very suspicious. It was a lot too good to be true."

"You didn't know?"

"Didn't know what?"

For a moment the Major looked at me as if he hardly believed in me. Then the leathery face folded up into a grin and the little duck's eyes positively twinkled.

"You must have been a bit hot under the collar at times," he said. "Fancy having the Hungarian Police giving you their special number one treatment to find out something you'd never been told about."

"Quite so," I said stiffly. "Well, now I think I'll see if my bed's still made up."

"Don't be stuffy," said the Major. "And I'm afraid you can't go to bed yet. There's a job to be done." He pottered off down the hall. I thought for a moment of standing on my dignity, but he never looked round, and after a moment I followed him.

We went into the Operations Room.

A tall man was sitting in the chair beside Lady's empty desk. There were other people at the back of the room, too, but for the moment I had no eyes for them. I was staring at the man.

I thought for a wild moment that it was Colin. He was the same build and had the same pleasant, knobbly face. But as soon as he turned to the light I saw that it was a stranger.

All the same, I had seen that face before.

"David Szormeny," said the Major. "Head of the Hungarian State."

"Former head," said Szormeny. "We can, I think, say that with safety now. Former head."

I listened, fascinated. It was the same molasses and sour cream voice that I had heard on the wireless, but a shade more human at first hand.

"If you will allow me, sir. This is the gentleman I spoke of, who will act as courier to you and your family until you reach England."

He introduced me, and now, for the first time, I took in the other people in the room. One was Madame Szormeny, a little fair-haired woman, of half her husband's size, but with a very friendly smile. And two good-looking children, a girl of about fourteen and a boy of twelve. They were both wearing mountaineering kit and looked as pleased as any couple of kids who have done something naughty and got the grown-ups on their side about it.

"You, too, came over last night?" asked Szormeny.

"Yes, sir," I said. "I'm afraid I had the advantage of your preparations. It was quite unintentional."

"I was able to give certain orders at the frontier that proved helpful," agreed Szormeny.

"If I might suggest it, sir," said Major Piper, "you have an early start this afternoon. Your host and hostess the Baron and Baronin Milo would wish to receive you. And then to bed."

He fairly shooed everyone out of the room, but a glint out of the corner of his eye told me to wait. I sat on the edge of a chair, half of me concentrating on keeping awake and the other half trying to sort things out.

It was nearly an hour before the Major came back. He seemed pleased with himself.

"Well," he said.

"Well?"

"You knew nothing of it?"

"Nothing at all."

"It was a well-kept secret." He said it unboastfully. As an art lover might appraise a masterpiece by a painter long dead.

"Do you mean to say that the whole business was designed

to get David Szormeny out of his country and over to the west?"

"Yes."

"The strike and all."

"The strike was our cover plan, yes. It served both purposes. To keep their minds off our real plan, and to enable certain steps to be taken."

I remembered what I had read.

"You mean that Szormeny was able to move his family up to the western frontier?"

"That and other things."

"And it was worth the sacrifice of Lady—and Gheorge and Lisa—and anyone else who may get hurt when the strike is put down."

The Major paused for a moment before replying. Then he said, "You don't win a chess match by hanging on to all your pieces. Szormeny's defection is probably the biggest smack in the eye for the Comintern since Tito. But it isn't checkmate. Just an exchange of pieces. We'd have liked to do it without giving them Lady, but we couldn't guarantee the strike, unless he went there in person. That was Szormeny's own personal view of the situation. In fact I believe you heard him give it."

"Yes," I said. "I heard his broadcast. I didn't understand it, of course."

"The final sentences—the ones about the long arm of Hungary stretching over the border. It could have been phrased in three pre-arranged ways. The way he actually used meant a straight exchange. Lady and a strike for himself and his family."

I thought about it for a bit. There didn't seem to be much to say. "You said that I could help?"

"We want you to look after Szormeny and his family until they reach England."

"That was to have been Colin's job."

"Yes. First impressions are the great thing. Treat them like royalty and you can't go wrong."

"I haven't much experience of escorting royalty," I said,

"but I'll do my best. Is it just to be opening doors and ordering meals and making conversation? Or do you expect any trouble?"

"I shouldn't think there'd be any trouble. No. The plain fact is we've caught them on the hop. It will take them quite a time to get reorganised. Of course, they'll get after him in the end. Wherever he goes. Trotsky thought he was safe after ten years in Mexico City. I can lend you a gun if you're nervous."

"I'm as nervous as a kitten," I said, "but I won't bother you for a gun. I've borrowed two in the last few weeks and they've neither of them done me a particle of good. I'll trust to my wits this time."

"You're learning," said the Major.

"I'm beginning to learn," I said, "among other things, what a blundering nuisance I've been. I pictured myself as a hero of romance, jumping in to the aid of his country. Whereas all I really did was to land with both feet into the middle of someone else's careful plans. It's a miracle I didn't do even more damage."

He didn't pretend not to understand me.

"I'm glad you didn't come to any real harm," he said. "And you did us one good turn. If any single man combined the brains and authority to put a spoke in our wheel it was Colonel Dru."

"He hit a telegraph post," I said. "Swerving to avoid a child."

"I read about it in the papers," said the Major. "I also happen to have had a message from Radk. You repaid us good for evil, there. My private opinion is that Lady was a little rough on you."

"No rougher than he was with himself."

"Oh, no. Quite so. An odd type. All scent and natty suitings on the outside and hard as steel inside." He added, inconsequentially, "My father, who was born Pfeiffer, was stationed at Constantinople before the first World War. I was quite young, of course, but I can remember being introduced to Enver. He and Lady had a great deal in common. I think I should get off to bed now. I'll have an Embassy car here at two o'clock. The train goes at half-past. There's a plane laid on for you at Klagenfurt."

In fact a thick mist put paid to our plane, and we went on by train to Paris, so I had Szormeny and his family to myself for nearly the whole of their first twenty-four hours in the western world.

I began to appreciate just why Colin had been laid on for the job. Szormeny had a little German and a working knowledge of Russian, but he was only comfortable in his native Hungarian. And how he wanted to talk!

If you've kept a guard on your lips for half a lifetime and suddenly find yourself free you are bound to let rip. Also I suppose that anyone who's taken a new and decisive step feels an urge to explain and rationalise his conduct. I listened hard, and made unobtrusive notes when I could.

The real trouble, I gathered, was that Szormeny had hitched his wagon to the wrong star at Moscow. This was an occupational risk with Comintern leaders. Not even the most thoughtful of them could forecast which light would wax in the Kremlin and which would wane. And Szormeny had remembered Rajk and Sakasits and had laid his careful plans accordingly.

He was comparatively young. He had free resources in Switzerland; resources which, by means which he explained to me, but which were too complicated for me to follow, he had increased during the years of his power in the Hungarian State. Also he had distant relatives in England who lived at a place which I found it extermely difficult to identify even when he spelt it out for me, but which turned out to be Kingston Bagpuize.

I jotted down what I could and, in my sleeping berth that night, put together my jottings into the form of rough notes. I also, when I got back, wrote a clear and connected account of my whole adventures. No one seemed to get very worked up about my adventures, but my notes went to the Cabinet.

We had an uneventful journey. Madame Szormeny knitted, her husband talked to me, and the two children behaved exactly like any other children on a long train journey.

There was a private plane at Orly. We took off at first light, and landed at Ferryfield a little over an hour later.

Why we didn't go straight to London Airport I have no idea, and the distinguished Foreign Office types must have left their beds very early to be on the Kent coast at that hour in the morning.

Colin would have been on Christian name terms with all of them, but they were just newspaper faces to me, and I handed my charges over to them, and they bowed and smiled and the Szormenys bowed and smiled, and I even did a bit of bowing and smiling myself; and then the big car doors slammed, and I declined to share a back seat with an Under-Secretary, and went off to find breakfast.

Over my breakfast I read all the papers I could lay hands on. There wasn't a word in any of them yet about Szormeny's defection. The situation, I gathered, was now under control. A number of agitators had been rounded up and the Peoples' Court would soon have the opportunity of showing how Hungary dealt with traitors.

One message stated that "A man called Lody, an ex-politician with several aliases," had been arrested.

It seemed a poor sort of epitaph.

I had to change trains twice before I got to London, and the third train I got into was packed with office workers. I squeezed into a first-class carriage. Everyone was very excited about something, and since Hungary came into it it occurred to me that the later editions might have got hold of the Szormeny story; but by listening and peering over people's shoulders I discovered that it was a Hungarian Soccer team which had played England the afternoon before. The referee, a Pole, had awarded a critical (and much criticised) penalty in the closing minutes from which the Hungarians had scored the only goal in the match.

"In Palmerston's day," said an old buffer in the

corner, "we wouldn't have stood for it. We should have sent a battleship."

I agreed with him heartily; but then blotted my copy-book by inquiring whether he suggested we should send a battleship to Hungary or Poland. This got me sent to Coventry for the rest of the journey.

I did not care greatly. Indeed, I found the whole atmosphere intensely reassuring.